COMPANIONS OF SAINT FRANCIS OF ASSISI

Brother Leo Remembers FRANCIS

Roderic Petrie, O.F.M.

Monica
Carocci

ST. ANTHONY MESSENGER PRESS

Cincinnati, Ohio

Cover illustration by Chris Sickels
Cover design by Constance Wolfer
Book design by Mary Alfieri
Electronic pagination and format by Sandy L. Digman

ISBN 0-86716-365-8

Published by St. Anthony Messenger Press
Printed in the U.S.A.

CONTENTS

INTRODUCTION

BROTHER LEO, A PRIEST OF ASSISI, joined Francis and the other friars in the very early days of the Order. Leo became a close companion of Francis, often performing the duties of a secretary, and would offer Mass for those of the group who, like Francis, were not ordained to the priesthood.

Along with two other early friars, Angelo and Rufino, Leo is believed to have written a collection of accounts of their experiences with Francis in those early days. Rufino's account of Francis is told in *The Autumn of Saint Francis of Assisi*. The following story draws upon some of those early episodes, but it is basically a work of fiction, presenting events that might have happened and words that might have been spoken, and a Francis that might have been.

CHAPTER
༄1༄

W E HAD SPENT THE NIGHT with the friars at
Montefalco. Early in the morning, the sun still
below the misty ridges of the Apennines to the East,
we followed the road that would lead us to Bevagna,
past Spello, and on to our destination, Saint Mary of
the Angels. Walking already for several hours, single
file, each immersed in his own thoughts and prayers,
and enjoying the beautiful day, Rufino called us to a
halt. We had elected Rufino to be our leader for the
day. My eyes had been following a hawk drifting idly
far above us riding the morning breeze, so I almost
bumped into Francis who walked in front of me.

"We'll stop under that big oak in the clearing there
to pray and to rest a bit," Rufino said. "Leo, pull our
Breviary out of your sack."

I took out the Breviary that I always pack when
traveling. Although we might claim exemption from
saying the psalms when traveling, Francis always
insisted that we stop to pray the Hours at the proper
times. So we sat down in the shade of the old oak to
recite Sext. Reciting psalms which we knew by heart,
we offered them up to God as songs of praise in this

open-air cathedral. As is usual in such a place, a few birds in the branches above accompanied us with their chirping.

As we prayed, the choir above us grew in numbers and volume. Not only were the branches filled with all kinds of birds, but the clearing around the tree began to fill as well. Our prayers came to an end, and the birds' songs, each according to its kind, became more fervent. Overcome with the wonder of the moment, we sat still, listening to the chorus of praise surrounding us.

Francis got to his feet and walked out a bit from the tree. Because the sun bothered his eyes he had his hood pulled over his head. He pushed the hood back, the better to see the number and variety of birds gathered around us. They did not fly away as they usually do at the approach of a human, although some hopped out of his way; and even those did not fly away when the hem of his habit brushed their backs.

His face aglow, as a contented man surrounded by family and friends, Francis spoke to them. "My little Brother and Sister Birds," he cried, to make himself heard. At once the birds became still. Many that perched in the tree flew down and gathered around him, large birds and small ones, some with brightly colored feathers, others as modest as nuns.

"Thank you," Francis began again, "for allowing us to join in your praises to God. The good God has blessed you with lovely voices and songs to sing. He clothes you with warm feathers and provides abundant food for you to eat. You need not spin nor reap, as we do. No, God fills all your needs, and asks only that you praise his goodness with your songs." With these words and others Francis preached to them, congratulating them for their service of the Lord and encouraging them to continue to praise God wherever they find themselves. The birds, meanwhile, listened attentively, some spreading their wings and bowing down to the earth. When he had finished preaching, Francis dismissed them, making the Sign of the Cross over them, and telling them to go throughout the countryside bringing the message of God's goodness. With a burst of song and the rush of wings, off they went in every direction, leaving a stillness that was as moving as their song.

"Did you see? Did you hear?" cried Francis. "Why have I never preached to our brother and sister creatures before? Doesn't Saint Paul tell us that they, too, all creation, mourn and struggle under the weight of sin, waiting to be released, along with us, when Jesus comes again? They need to be encouraged as much as we. They need to be reminded of God's love for them as much as we."

It was after that day at Bevagna when Francis preached to the birds that he would preach to other creatures as well: to creatures animate and inanimate, to flocks and herds or a single hawk or hare, to trees, water and stones. Ever after he took to heart the Lord's instruction to preach the Good News to all of creation.

So then, Brother Bonaventure, this is the type of recollection of the deeds and words of our father Francis that you asked me to compile and send to you to help with the Life of Saint Francis which you intend to write. Some years ago, twenty years after our father Francis' death, Brother Rufino and I, along with Brother Angelo, who wrote it all down, gathered our recollections and sent them to Brother Crescentius of Jesi who, as you are now, was the General Minister at that time. He gave our writings to Brother Thomas of Celano who incorporated much of what we remembered into a book, which I am sure you have. What happened to those writings of ours I have no idea. Perhaps you can discover them. But in case you cannot, I will try to recall for you some of those remarkable events of the early days of our Order, while Francis still lived, as you asked.

Please forgive my poor penmanship. My hand now shakes a bit, my sight is not as keen, thirty-five years after Francis' death, and perhaps my memory as well is shaky and not as keen, but I hope not. How could I forget?

I knew Francis and his family all of my life. Like him, I was born and grew up in Assisi. But unlike him, I was poor. My father was a weaver, like Francis' grandfather, and he worked for Signore Bernardone, Francis' father. Indeed, so did my mother, working on hand-looms at home, and I and my older brothers and sisters (we were six) all learned early on to weave and embroider so we could add to the family income.

When I say "I knew Francis," that is not to say that we were close friends. He was four or five years older than I, so I knew his younger brother Angelo much better. But even though Francis was never one to choose friends according to their social or financial status, still his friends were older and they did not want younger brothers trailing after them. Francis had many friends for he was fun to be with, lighthearted and gregarious. Any party was sure to be a success if Francis Bernardone attended. And later, in his teenage years and older, he might lead a group of friends through the streets singing songs, maybe serenading one of the boys' sweethearts. Innocent fun. And the adults all liked him, too, for he was respectful, not a bad influence at all. But he was something of a worry for his father and mother, especially his father, who longed to see his son settle down, preferably in the family business of cloth merchandizing.

From time to time my own father would come home with a story of how Francis could not say "no" to a beggar who might come into the shop. Evidently the beggars of the town, whenever Francis was alone and his father was occupied elsewhere, would use the opportunity to ask for a coin "for the love of God," knowing that Francis could not resist that simple petition. They knew better than to try that line on Signore Bernardone, a tightfisted businessman. But his son was another matter. If some poor mother could persuade her child to shiver a bit from the cold or shed a tear, she would get the best cloth at the cheapest price. These things made Francis' father despair that his son would ever make a successful merchant.

And yet Signore Bernardone was not an unkind man. Although he wanted hard work done for the price he paid, he was good enough to my father, and when I decided that I would like to study for the priesthood, he helped me pay for my classes with the priests at St. George. That is really when I got to know Francis better, when his father sent him there as well to learn to read and write.

I have to admit that Francis was not interested in the intricacies of Latin grammar or the poets. When he felt the urge to hike in the hills with some friends, he wouldn't let schoolwork stand in his way. Many a time I had to review the previous day's lesson with him before the teacher opened the door to let us into the classroom. So this was the way Francis' life seemed to be developing: the likeable son of a well-to-do merchant, a young man who would never, it seemed, settle down to make something of himself. It was becoming more evident to everyone, and especially to his father, I suppose, astute businessman that he was, that Francis' talents were not in merchandizing. Whatever talents he had, his father feared that, left to himself, Francis would in no time run the shop and the family fortune into the ground.

Then an intriguing possibility arrived in the person of a messenger from Walter of Brienne who was leading the pope's forces in the south to break the stranglehold the emperor had on the papal states. All the towns and cities loyal to the pope were asked to send soldiers and knights to Apulia for a forthcoming battle.

Perhaps this was the solution to the dilemma of what to do with Francis: if not a merchant, then a knight. Certainly the life of a knight seemed more appropriate for Francis who liked a good time and to be the generous gentleman! And a touch of nobility would further the family's standing in the commune as well. Hadn't Francis often boasted at his parties that he would one day be a noble lord? Yes, that had all gotten back to his indulgent father's ears. Well, here was the chance that Providence seemed to be providing. Francis would go off to Apulia, win his spurs as a knight and return to Assisi as Sir Francis, son of Pietro Bernardone.

Nothing was too good for Francis the knight. The finest charger (a gentle horse, to be sure, because Francis was not much of a horseman), the best armor (a good buy from a traveling Spanish merchant) and a wardrobe at wholesale price. Francis looked like the noblest of knights.

It was early in the year 1205, the day after the Feast of Epiphany. Nine knights and perhaps twice as many yeomen gathered in the piazza of San Rufino. They would travel first to Spoleto where they would join recruits from other towns and cities of the area, then continue on to Apulia. Although it was a cold day and snow had fallen farther up on Mount Subasio, it was clear and sunny in Assisi. The bishop came out to bless them while many of us looked on. Some women leaned out of upstairs windows of the homes around the square to wave their final good-byes to a son, a friend. Then the troop clattered down the street and out the gate leading to Foligno and south. I have to admit that I was a bit envious of such splendor and bravery as they passed me, sparkling and proud in the sunlight, but I was happy, too, happy for Francis that he had found his place in life.

Three days later Francis returned. I had been visiting some friends who lived outside the walls and was walking along the road, about to enter the gate, when out of the deep shadow of some trees stepped a figure leading a limping horse.

"Francis," I whispered rather stupidly, "is that you?"

"Yes, Leo, the conquering hero returns home. You haven't seen my father, have you? Did he leave on that trip to Genoa that he was planning?"

"No, Francis, I haven't seen him. My father mentioned this morning that Signore Bernardone left yesterday and plans to be away until the week before Ash Wednesday. Are you all right? You're not hurt or anything, are you?"

"No, Leo, thanks. I'm all right. I'm going home now. I'll talk to you later." And with that Francis went off down the street, leading the footsore horse behind him.

It wasn't until years later that I learned what happened. Francis and I were seated in the stillness on a large rock far above Assisi watching the sun sink below the mountains opposite us. Darkness was filling up the valley, brimming over to touch us where we sat. Here and there a far-off fire sparkled in the darkness, a farmer burning some rubbish. A woman's voice drifted up to us from somewhere below, a mother calling her children to supper. The emerging stars and a half moon gave scant light on the path behind us that led up to the hermitage where we were staying with Brother Bernard and Brother Giles.

"Do you remember, Leo," Francis asked, "the night I came back from Spoleto? It was a night just like this."

I nodded my head in the darkness but didn't say anything. The last bits of orange and gold dripped out of the clouds over yonder and disappeared below the horizon.

"I had waited for more than an hour outside the gate that night until it was dark, as it is now, before venturing into town. I knew that I was doing the right thing, that I did not belong in Apulia with the army, but I was ashamed, too, to return home. Ashamed more for my father and mother, I think, than for myself, because that was one more thing that I did not succeed in. My parents wanted me to be happy, to be settled, to be successful at something, at anything, but I wasn't any of those: not successful, not settled, not happy.

"The venture had started out well enough. In fact, I was looking forward to a battle and the chance to prove to Walter of Brienne and to myself that I should be a knight. I've not told this to anyone before, Leo, but the night before leaving I had a remarkable dream. In my dream I saw my home in Assisi, but it was very different from what it really was. The house was far more grand and impressive, like a castle, and all over the walls were shields, weapons and what I took to be the spoil from battles. The shields and weapons I understood belonged to knights who were in my service. Seeing all of that, I knew in my heart that I was called to be a great lord and would win my spurs and much honor during the campaign. So when you saw us off that day, I might not have been a knight, although I was dressed like one, but I was convinced that on my return I would be a knight in truth.

"We made good time, joined by other recruits as we went along, so that by the time we got to Spoleto, the gathering area, we were several hundred. Our own group from Assisi was given an area under some trees on the edge of a farmer's wheat field that he had just harvested, but I wandered about among the other groups looking, truthfully, for likely knights who might be future comrades and to see if I could recognize any of the emblems on the shields that I had seen in my dream. When the commander of the group announced that we would be early on the road the next day, I was ready for a good night's sleep because the day had been a long one. As soon as I lay down, I was instantly asleep.

"During the night I had that dream again. The very same dream, Leo: my home, larger and more grand than it really was, the walls covered with shields and weapons, the corners stacked with booty won in war. But this time I did not feel the same contentment and pride that I had before. In fact I was uneasy with what I saw. Then the Lord spoke to me."

"You're sure it was the Lord?" I asked.

"I'm positive it was, Leo. I knew it."

"What did he say?"

"He spoke to me by name. 'Francis,' he said, 'is it better to serve the lord or the servant?'

"'The lord,' I answered. 'Then why do you serve the servant?' I awoke at once. It was the middle of the night, the moon more than half way across the sky, the stars bright as candles. I was wide awake at once, Leo. And do you know, I had within me not only the conviction that it truly was God who spoke to me, but I also knew I did not belong there. I did not belong in Apulia. I belonged in Assisi, back home. I had no idea why I should return home, what I would do when I got there, but that didn't matter. Have you ever had that experience when you have been praying about something that suddenly the answer is there clearly in your heart and you know it is right? Maybe you weren't even thinking of the problem at that moment, but there the answer is all at once and you know that it is correct. God speaks to our hearts at those moments; not with words, but with truth."

Again, in the darkness, I nodded my head, for I had known those moments, too.

Francis continued, "I gathered together my armor, my sword, my duffel bag of clothing, and in the darkness I searched out Giovanni Polidoro. You remember him. A very fine fellow, and a knight, a *real* knight, but his family couldn't outfit him like my father had done for me. I woke him up and I said: 'Giovanni, I want to trade my belongings for yours because I've decided to go home. You will be able to use these things far better than I.' Well, he didn't want to do it. At first he tried to talk me out of returning home. Then he didn't want to take my armor, horse and all. But when I told him that if he didn't take it I would just leave it all there in the field for anyone who wanted it, he gave in. So that night when you saw me return I wore his armor and had his horse. The poor thing was so worn out that I didn't have the heart to ride on it; it might have died on the way home.

"So that is why I came home from Spoleto, Leo. The Lord directed me back to Assisi. But to what, I had no idea. There was, however, the confidence that I was called to serve not an earthly lord, but the Lord of heaven and earth; and that any followers I might have might be noble in their manner of life rather than in their social status. You helped me, Leo, to give my life over to God and to do his will."

"I did?" I said, a little startled. "How?"

"We used to come up here together to these caves," Francis recalled. "Remember? You were so patient with me, waiting outside somewhere while I would go into a cave and spend time praying, asking God to show me the way I was to go, asking God what he wanted of me."

"Well, while you were in one of those caves praying for guidance, Francis, I was doing the same thing outside. I guess God heard both our prayers," I said.

"Yes, but not at once. We were on our way together

to visit one of my father's tenants down in the valley by Rivo Torto. I had to collect the rent and you came along. When we got as far as San Damiano it began to rain so hard that we ran in there for shelter. Remember?"

"Yes, even so we got wet," I added, "because the roof leaked so badly. We decided we would spend some time in prayer until the rain stopped, so you went over to the big crucifix that hung down over the altar, while I stayed in the back. I never told you this before, Francis, but I was going through my own difficult time with God then. I had to make the decision whether to ask the bishop to admit me to Holy Orders or to give up my studies and maybe consider the vocation of marriage. It was that day that the decision to continue my studies became a conviction in my heart. In a way, I think my decision had something to do with you because I recall being in the back of the chapel while you were under the crucifix, the rain dripping in through the roof all around you while you seemed lost in conversation with Jesus. The sight of that, I think, moved me to want to give myself to God as a priest, to be as dedicated to God as you seemed to be."

"That is curious, Leo, because it was at that time that the Lord gave me my direction.

"The Lord spoke to me from the cross that day as clearly as I am speaking to you right now. 'Francis,' he said, 'as you see, my church is falling into ruin. Rebuild my church.' As you said, the roof leaked badly, the plaster was falling off the walls, the stones in the walls were loose. It certainly had become a ruin, and needed fixing. What I had been looking for was suddenly there for me. I would become a rebuilder of rundown churches. There were plenty of them around Assisi, places where God could not be fittingly worshiped anymore because of their squalor or lack of repair. That, it seemed to me, was something worthwhile and within my abilities."

That is what Francis did. But his zeal for his new vocation and some poor judgment got him into trouble. While his father was away Francis took the opportunity to leave home and live at the Church of San Damiano in a little room that the priest there made available to him. But when he left home he took with him a good amount of cloth. How he excused that to himself, I don't know; perhaps he looked on it as an inheritance from his father that he would not get in the future, perhaps as payment for his efforts at the shop, I don't know. But he loaded a horse with some bolts of cloth, rode to Foligno and there he sold it all: cloth and horse. Returning to San Damiano, Francis proudly offered the generous sum to the priest for the rebuilding of the chapel. The priest, no fool, would not touch the money, dubious of Francis' right to the money and fearful of Signore Bernardone's wrath. So Francis tossed the sack of money on a window ledge and said nothing more about it.

But then there was the devil to pay! Francis' father of course loved his son very much, doted on him, but was at his wit's end about how to bring Francis around to do what any self-respecting son of a businessman should do: get down to business. Whenever Signore Bernardone came across Francis in the streets begging stones for his work at San Damiano, he would become furious.

"A stone? You want a stone?" And he would hurl a stone at Francis. Once he grabbed Francis by the hair and, cursing, dragged him back to his home where he locked him in a closet. "You can stay in there," he shouted, "until you learn some sense!" But as soon as he was gone Lady Pica, Francis' mother, let him out and, of course, Francis returned to San Damiano. Not only the neighbors knew of the father's frustration and rage, but the whole commune enjoyed the drama.

Clearly something had to be done to settle the matter, so Signore Bernardone played the only card he had left. He took his son to court. But even then Francis eluded him, for Francis, living at San Damiano, claimed that he had given himself over to the Lord's service and therefore no longer was bound by the civil courts. God was his judge! Not to be outdone, his father hailed Francis before the bishop and demanded justice: restitution for the cloth that Francis had taken to Foligno and sold.

While standing in the courtyard of the bishop's residence, Francis and his father were joined by a knot of interested onlookers. The bishop asked Francis: "Is it true, my son, that you took bolts of cloth from your father's shop, carried them off to Foligno and sold them?"

"Yes, bishop," admitted Francis, "I did. I'm not sure

now why I did that except probably I have been so used to being able to buy and pay for whatever I wanted that I must have thought I could give some money to old Father Vittorio down there and he would hire someone to fix up the church. It seemed like a good idea at the time, but then Father Vittorio wouldn't accept the money."

"Your father did not give you permission to sell the cloth nor, having sold it, to give away the money, Francis, so you owe him restitution," the bishop told him.

"Your grace, when the priest would not accept the money, I tossed the purse onto a windowsill there at the chapel. It has been there all this time gathering dust like the dust it is made of. During the weeks that I have been living there at San Damiano people have been supplying me with everything I need for the work. I don't need money at all. In fact, it gets in the way. Look at all the trouble it is causing right now. I want nothing to do with money; not now, not ever again. I've honestly been meaning to give it back, but I guess I have been avoiding my father."

Then, speaking even more loudly so that those around could hear him, Francis turned to his father and said, "Father, I know that you have tried to do what you thought best for me. But I have another Father, our Father in heaven, who knows what is truly best for me. From now on I will call no one father but him, and I will trust him to provide my needs, even to the clothes on my back." And with that Francis suddenly took off the clothing he had on, right in front of us all, and lay the pile at his father's feet. The bishop, red-faced, whipped off his own cloak and threw it around Francis. A few in the crowd gathered there snickered, not knowing how to react to such a scene. But Francis did. He stepped free of the bishop's cloak and, head up, walked out the city gate wearing nothing but a smile.

Later I heard that a friend gave him a simple tunic such as peasants wear in the fields, and that he made his way to the Benedictine Abbey of San Benedetto up on the mountainside to seek shelter and, I suppose, to think things out. But his reception there was not all that warm from the abbot, who perhaps feared the displeasure of Signore Bernardone. Francis was told that he could help out in the kitchen, but was offered nothing to eat and had to sleep by the hearth, so the next day he continued on over the mountain to Gubbio where, for six months he volunteered his efforts in a hospital for lepers.

My theology teacher, Father Mario, said to me one day at the end of our session, "Francis Bernardone is back, you know." I didn't know. But I was glad to hear it. "When did he come back? Where is he?"

"Just the day before yesterday. He's back at San Damiano, working on the church again," Father Mario replied.

And coming out of St. George into the sunlight, there Francis was, standing on one of the steps of the fountain in the piazza. He had a few people gathered around him and he was talking to them. Preaching to them, really. Even from the doorway I could hear him for he had a voice that carried, a pleasant voice, a voice for singing.

"Jesus did not take on our flesh to make us his slaves," he was saying, "but to make us his brothers and sisters. We are of the same family with him. His father is our father and his mother Mary is our mother as well. Certainly he was begotten and we were made, so Jesus is God of true God, but nonetheless we are of his family, adopted sons and daughters through our baptism, and sharing in the same human nature. So why should we fear our brother Jesus, and shouldn't we love our brother Jesus with all our hearts? If we love those of our own families should we not love Jesus even more since he, too, is our brother? All of you know how I have been foolish, wasting my life on nothing, but now I want to spend my days praising our Father in heaven and the brother he has given us, Jesus, who is our Lord. May God give you each the will to do the same, and the blessing of his peace."

Francis spied me coming down the steps of the church and crossed over to me. "Hello, Leo," he said. I was aware that he looked at the shaved circle on the top of my head, my tonsure, so I answered his unspoken question.

"Yes, I took Holy Orders from the bishop. I'm to be ordained deacon in September (it was only July) and a priest in March. It's good to see you, Francis. We've missed you around town. You look fit." And he did. Maybe he was thinner than he had been, but he had never been robust. He had on some kind of homespun tunic of undyed wool, a leather belt around him and a hood that covered his shoulders, but no shoes or sandals. It was his eyes that held my attention, for although I remembered them as black, there seemed to be a welcome in them, and to look into them was like looking into a well that opened to the depths of eternity. Here was a man at peace with himself and with the world, I thought.

"Yes, Leo, I'm well. And why shouldn't I be? The brothers at the leprosarium in Gubbio where I have been the past six months made sure that I ate well. And Father Vittorio down at San Damiano is always pressing food on me. But that has to stop. I can't let him provide for me. I am able to work, thank God, and when I don't have work that pays anything, like now, then I should ask at the Lord's table like other beggars do."

After that I would see him from time to time with a bowl in his hands, eating something that he had begged. I recall one evening that he came to our door; there was a knock and I went to answer it.

"Francis," I said, glad to see him. "What can I do for you? Come in."

"No, thank you, Leo," he murmured. "I have come to beg some food for the love of God. I was ashamed to come down this street and have been avoiding it because your father works for mine and you know me so well. It's easier to beg from someone I don't know. It took me three times to come to the door before I could knock on it."

"Of course we have some food for you," I said, hoping in my heart that I was right. Sometimes mother could give a sharp answer if I caught her in a bad mood, but that evening she couldn't have been nicer. She filled his bowl with thick soup and gave him a large slab of bread freshly baked, and feeling motherly I guess, gave Francis a peck on the cheek, asking him to pray for her boy who would be ordained a priest in a few months. Left alone, Francis whispered to me that he could not possibly eat all that mother had pressed upon him. He urged me to share his beggar's meal, which I did, to give him company. I must say that my mother's soup had never tasted so good nor the bread any better. It was a meal I will always remember.

Not being able simply to pay for the repairs of the church, Francis had set about doing the work himself. He was far from a professional stonemason, to be sure, but he and most of us in Assisi were reasonably capable from our experience of building up the city walls when we became an independent commune. Later he told me that when he soon ran out of available stones there on the property, he had no feeling of shame to go about in Assisi asking people for stones. In fact, he made a game of it, since it was for such a good purpose, and he would say: "For a stone for San Damiano, a blessing. For two stones, two blessings." So he had an ample supply of stones, mortar, whatever he needed, and we who watched what he was doing gave as we would to a good-natured simpleton.

To some he was not just a strange young man who

had taken it into his head to rebuild an old chapel and live like a tramp when he had a perfectly nice home of his own. To some, he was a challenge, an itch to the conscience. Like Bernard di Quintavalle. A year or so older than Francis, a knight, well off, a member of an old family hereabouts, he started out going down to San Damiano to give Francis a hand with the work and he ended up selling his house, his property, and giving all the money away. Then, to everyone's amazement he, too, went to live at the chapel. Then there was a third, a young man from one of the farms in the area. Everyone called him Simple, or Giovanni the Simple, for he was that. And what a worker! He worked twice as hard as either Francis or Bernard, and Francis told me later that he wondered if the citizens of Assisi could hear Simple snore at night for he worked hard at that, too.

Nor could I get out of my own head the memory of Francis kneeling in front of that old crucifix in San Damiano, the rain coming through the roof, and he oblivious to it, lost in conversation with God. My own vocation to serve God was somehow linked to his, but what did that mean for me? I did not want to be a stonemason. I did not want to spend my priesthood rebuilding run-down churches.

From San Damiano Francis, Bernard and John moved on to another little chapel: San Pietro della Spina down in the valley. There a sad thing happened. Simple John, who thought that Francis was a saint and used to imitate everything Francis did, the way he did it, so that he, too, would be holy, became ill and died.

Francis could not have mourned a blood brother more. "In fact," he said to me, "John was more dear to me than any brother of blood for not my parents but God gave him to me."

Then Bernard and Francis went on to another little chapel, one belonging to the Benedictine Monks, St. Mary of the Angels, deep in the woods below Assisi. This they also rebuilt and they made some huts among the trees where they lived and spent their time in prayer.

I had already been ordained for several months and was serving the people at St. Mary's in Assisi, when one day in February I went down to visit Francis and Bernard. To my surprise there were two other companions there, bringing their number to four. One I knew at once from Assisi, Peter Catanii, recently back from his studies at the university. The other I didn't know. His name was Giles and I learned that he was from one of the poor farming families working on an estate down the valley. It was evident from the way he spoke that he was uneducated, but it also became evident that he had a quick mind and a tongue to match it.

Francis had asked me to say Mass for them there in the little chapel they had repaired, so I readily agreed. Until he died Francis always considered it a great loss if he could not attend Mass each day. That particular day was the feast of Saint Matthias, I recall. The Gospel, of course, was about the sending forth of the apostles to bring the Good News, without making provision for their needs and relying on God to provide for them.

When the Mass was over, Francis asked me to explain the Gospel. Although he understood Latin fairly well, he was no student of it, as I've said, so I suppose he wasn't sure whether he had grasped everything. After I explained how Jesus sent his friends out to preach and cautioned them to let God provide for them and not worry about what to eat or where to stay, he fairly shouted to all of us: "That's it! That is what the Lord has been trying to tell me. This is what I want to do! When God spoke to me and told me to rebuild his church, he wasn't speaking of San Damiano and other tumbled-down chapels. As good as that work is, God meant for us to rebuild the CHURCH, to bring the message of God's love and forgiveness to everyone. Yes, I understand now. We have to start at once!"

Whenever Francis was excited his whole body participated. Now he was fairly dancing around the small chapel. He grabbed a bit of rope they had been using there in the church and, taking off his leather belt, he tied the rope about his waist.

"No belt, God says. No money. No shoes. Well, we don't have to worry about those, do we? We have neither. Tomorrow morning we'll begin to carry out the Lord's directions. We will pair off and go in opposite directions, preaching to everyone to be converted and make changes in their lives. Just as Jesus did! Won't that be fun? Aren't we lucky to be able to do it?"

"Francis," I found myself saying, caught up in the excitement of the moment, "may I go, too?"

"Oh, Leo," he said, "I have been hoping that you

would want to join us, but no. Not now, anyhow. You are in the service of the bishop here and you have your parents to think of. No, you must think about it, pray about it. We will return here by Palm Sunday. Then we will talk about it again. This is too sudden."

"But Francis, I think I have been thinking about it. That is, *God* has been thinking about it, for a long time. You're right, though, I need to pray more about it, maybe talk to the bishop and also to my family. They have to be willing. While you are away I will pray that God will open hearts to you."

The next morning, after Mass and a visit to old Signora Lombardi, I hurried down to St. Mary of the Angels to see Francis and the others off. But when I arrived no one was there; they had already left. As I stood there outside the little chapel and saw the huts made of branches and mud, the stark poverty of the place, I was filled with a deep sense of peace as though I had been far from home for a long time but had returned to where I belonged. I knew that this was where I was meant to be. I knew that when Palm Sunday came I would join Francis, Bernard, Peter and Giles. I knew it. And that is what happened.

The journey from Bevagna took a bit longer than expected that day. After Francis preached to the birds and accused himself of being remiss in not preaching to fellow creatures before this, as the Lord Jesus had instructed us, Francis would call us to stop while he preached to a hawk, a grove of olive tees, a thorn bush. Rufino, who continued to lead us, did his best to set a pace that would get us to St. Mary of the Angels by nightfall. Pausing only to pray and to rest a bit, to sip some water, we trudged on. A Roman legion would have been proud of us. Even so, when we arrived at St. Mary's, shadows were already deep there in the valley below Assisi.

We were seven: Francis and Peter Catanii, John and Angelo, Rufino and Anthony of Portugal, and me. In the gloom it was nonetheless evident that a fence had been put up in our absence to enclose the little chapel of St. Mary of the Angels, the friars' huts and the vegetable gardens. A good idea, I thought, because sometimes we had no privacy from the people coming to see Francis or just to see how we lived.

A friar at the gate let us in at the first knock, overjoyed to see Francis and us and was about to call all the friars when Francis calmed him, saying there would be time in the morning to greet everyone, that we were exhausted and needed only a place to sleep. So when he led us to some huts near the gate, we said goodnight to each other and, falling on a mat in the dark hut, I immediately fell into a deep and untroubled sleep.

But I awakened to anything but an untroubled morning. "Who taught you to live in a palace?" Crash! The voice was unmistakably Francis'. "Next you will want to be lords and expect poor folk to serve you!" Crash! I ran outside the hut and there, behind the chapel was a building that had not been there when we left. On top of it was Francis, throwing roof tiles to the ground below. "I'll level this faster than it went up," he cried, and down came another tile. Some friars were dancing about below to avoid the rain of tiles while trying to explain to him.

"It isn't ours, Father Francis," they wailed. "It belongs to the Commune of Assisi. It isn't our building that you are tearing down."

"It isn't ours?" asked Francis, pausing in his patently enjoyable work of dismantling the roof.

"No, Father Francis," explained Brother Guido, the superior of St. Mary of the Angels. "The mayor of Assisi came one day to tell us that he and the people of Assisi were concerned for the infirm friars who would be here at Chapter time. It was not right, they said, that the sick should be exposed to rain, to cold, to the night air, so they decided to build a house for them. I told them that, as kind as their offer was and as generous their concern, we could not accept a house of stone and mortar, such as this, for it was far better than what we poor friars could own. He made it clear to me, and he said I should make it clear to you, Father Francis, that the house was not to be owned by the friars. The house would be owned and maintained by the Commune of Assisi which would be glad to lend it to us."

"Oh," said Francis, replacing a tile, rather reluctantly, I thought, to its place. "Well, in that case, I acted too quickly and have injured another's property. I'm sorry. It's just that," he continued, standing up and working his way carefully to the ladder he had placed against the building, "I have heard, even in the Holy Land, how Lady Poverty is no longer welcome among the fri-

28

ars as she once was."

"That might be true enough, Father Francis," Guido agreed, "but Lady Poverty is still mistress here at St. Mary of the Angels, as you will see. Come down. We want to celebrate your safe return. We've missed you."

Of all those places that Francis loved, none could be called home for him except St. Mary of the Angels. For Francis it was the site of Jacob's ladder, it was where one might see angels ascending and descending, as our Lord told Saint Philip. Had Francis seen angels there at that little chapel? I don't know. But I do know that he was convinced that indeed angels abounded there. Many times he cautioned us, his early companions, that we should never give up that chapel, for he called it our mother church. If someone should drive us from the door, he would say, we should climb back in through a window. And so the chapel of St. Mary's, so dear to Francis, still holds a privileged place in the hearts of all his followers.

That is why, as magnificent as the sanctuary built by Brother Elias in Assisi might be, although it is where Francis' remains lie buried, the Chapters of the Order meet at St. Mary's for that is where his heart was. It was in this little chapel that Francis received the inspiration from the Lord to go out with his first friars and preach the gospel. It was always here that we returned to tell the wonders God had worked through us.

It is here that Sister Clare came that evening, so long ago now, to become a follower of the poor Christ, as Francis had done. It is here that Francis gave over the leadership of the brothers and appointed Peter Catanii to be the General Minister. And it is under this chapel that Peter lies buried, dead after only a year.

It is here that Jesus told Francis to ask the lord pope for a plenary indulgence for any of the faithful who would come to St. Mary of the Angels, confess their sins and receive the Eucharist.

Here Francis rolled in rose bushes to rid himself of temptations, and the roses, now without thorns, bloom to this day. And so many other memories are a part of this special place. Is it any wonder that every friar, of whatever nationality, considers St. Mary of the Angels to be his homeland? If never here, they long to see it. Once here, all long to return.

On one occasion, in the dead of winter, Francis had gone to Foligno to preach. I was his companion. Returning in the afternoon, I was walking ahead along the frozen path. The freezing wind off Mount Subasio swirled snow around us, skittering it along the ground. We had our hoods pulled over our heads and mantels wrapped tightly around us. Perhaps the allure of a warm hearth and a hot bowl of soup made me walk a bit more quickly. Francis noticed it.

"Leo," he said, interrupting my conjecture as to whether there might also be a little wine to accompany the soup. "Do you know what should make us perfectly happy?"

Well, I had a pretty good idea of what would make *me* very happy at that moment, but I answered: "No, Francis, what?"

"Leo, little lamb of God"—Francis liked to tease me that I was hardly as ferocious a lion as my name implied—"if after our sermons hundreds of people tell us that they have repented of their sins and they acclaim us the best preachers they have ever heard; if the bishop of that place should invite us to preach to his priests and the lord of the castle loads us down with cakes and skins of wine for the brothers; if the people weep and lament when we leave that place, Leo, little lamb of God, note it well, that is not perfect happiness."

We walked on a bit farther. The top of Mount Subasio was no longer visible and the flank of the mountain was becoming white. I shivered with the cold and thought again of the warm fire, the welcoming friars awaiting us at St. Mary's.

"Leo," Francis said again. "If because of our preaching the lord pope should ask us to Rome to preach to the cardinals and all his household; if because of our way of life all the princes and lords of Christendom would live at peace with each other; if the wealthy bankers and tradesmen would share their wealth with the poor; if we were honored and acclaimed by the whole world, note it well, Leo, that is not perfect happiness."

The freezing wind changed direction, now blowing snow into our eyes and wrapping our habits around our legs, making walking even more difficult. I could barely restrain myself from running the last mile to St. Mary's, to the warm fire, some hot soup and some snug blankets.

"Little lamb, my brother Leo," Francis continued through chattering teeth, "if when we arrive at St. Mary's and ring the bell at the gate the Brother Porter opens it but a crack and tells us to go away for we are lazy louts looking to live on the alms given to worthy and poor friars, and then closes and bars the door, that is perfect happiness."

"But when he sees it is us, Francis and Leo, he will let us in right away and will feel sorry he treated us so," I objected.

"Not so, Leo," Francis continued. "For if we continue to knock and say: 'For the love of God, Brother Porter, open the gate for us. We are your brothers Francis and Leo,' he will say to us that we are impostors trying to gain entry where we do not belong. And when we cry louder and bang on the gate, if he comes out with a club and beats us, rolling us in the snow, leaving us bruised and numb from the cold, write it down and remember that this is perfect happiness."

I could now make out the fence at St. Mary of the Angels through the snow. No longer was I so sure I wanted to get there for often things Francis said seemed to come true.

"What are you telling me?" I shouted above the wind, hardly able to speak I was so cold. "How can such treatment make me happy?"

"Little lamb of God, dear Leo," answered Francis, "it is not enough that we go about preaching to others the sufferings of Jesus, bringing pious people to tears because Jesus was rejected, scorned and beaten. We must follow in his footsteps. And when we are chosen to receive the same treatment as he, then that is our greatest reward and highest honor. What greater happiness could one want than to have the same reception as one's master? Our Lord received not acclaim and honors, but disdain and a beating. If we are true disciples should we be content to be honored and applauded because we merely tell others about him?"

"I guess you're right, Francis," I agreed.

"Come on then," he shouted. "Let's ring the bell at the gate to see if our brother will give us a proper welcome deserving of a follower and servant of the poor Christ," and he began to run the distance to the gate. "Let's claim our welcome, whatever it might be."

And I, like a fool, took off after him, running through the snow, shouting: "Wait for me!" I confess that although I was not altogether sure I wanted a surly brother to answer our call, I was so happy to be running with Francis to receive whatever awaited us.

CHAPTER

~2~

SOME OF THESE MEMORIES come to mind readily because the events impressed me very much at
the time. Other things that happened only revealed
their importance at a later date. Two of these were the
gift to Francis and the friars of a mountain retreat, and
another was the fourth council held at St. John
Lateran.

As it comes back to me now, we had an early spring
in 1213 after a rather mild winter. Usually in the spring
roads are all but impassable because of the mud, but
that year Francis sent out friars early to preach so that
summer found them even beyond the Alps. The terrifying tales of being beaten and abused became less fre-
quent as the friars returned and told of their successes
because the name of the Order, and Francis' reputation,
too, were becoming better known.

By May of that year some friars who were preaching in the villages of the Apennines in the region of San
Marino responded to the invitation of Count Orlando
da Chiusi that they visit his family castle and his household at San Leo. He had heard much about their
preaching and wished to hear them himself.

Count Orlando was a pious and good man, kind to his tenants and conscientious about their spiritual welfare as well. Going to his castle, the friars were received warmly by all, especially by the count, eager to hear more of how these friars lived and about Francis. Simply said, Francis' love for God and his love for prayer, as he learned of them from the friars, moved Count Orlando to a generous act.

His estates contained a mountain, the top of which was nearly inaccessible, a place of tumbled boulders, deep crevices and thick forest. It is called La Verna. This mountaintop Count Orlando offered to Francis and the friars as a place of prayer and retreat. No document was given at the time for Francis might reject the offer, not wishing that any place be considered as belonging to us. But when the friars, on their return, told Francis of the offer, somewhat to the surprise of all, he accepted the gift. Only later, after their father's death, did the later counts of Chiusi confirm in writing their father's generosity. I mention this now because of what must be said later of the miraculous event that happened there at La Verna eleven years later, when Francis received the wounds of our Savior, and I was privileged to be there with him at the time.

Another event that had more importance than I thought at the time was the council held at the Lateran in 1215. The announcement of the council had been going on for several months, of course. Archbishops, bishops, abbots, theologians had been finding their way to Rome for weeks. Some traveled through the

Umbrian Valley, sometimes choosing to stop in Assisi rather than Perugia, where innkeepers are apt to take advantage of the unwary. Too, many wanted to visit St. Mary of the Angels to see for themselves how the friars lived and maybe meet Francis as well.

The lord Pope Innocent had announced the council to bring about some needed reforms in the Church. I won't mention here the pitiful conditions in many a diocese because of neglect, the lack of education for priests, the lack of respect for the Eucharist and other sad wounds to the body of the Church. Enough to say that the Church had grown cold and needed to be revived.

In early October a messenger from the pope came to St. Mary of the Angels looking for Francis. His Holiness desired that Francis come to Rome for the council. The invitation was an honor, to be sure, but I learned later that the pope had invited other heads of religious orders as well, so the honor was going to be shared by many.

We have a saying: "All roads lead to Rome." It is true, I suppose, for all the good roads, the major roads, were built by the Romans. For me, I have no interest in going to Rome. At one time, yes, I admit I desired to see it. Well, I went, I saw it, and that once was enough. Granted, one should visit the tombs of the apostles; I have done that and I enjoyed the privilege. One might enjoy seeing the remains of the ancient city, which I have done. But why anyone would choose to live there is beyond me. In spring the Tiber overflows and floods the low areas where the poor live. In summer the heat is like the heat from hell's fires, and mosquitoes torment everyone. The winter is damp, and at all seasons the city is stuffed with people and bad odors. No, I prefer my own Assisi and the valley of Umbria.

But when the messenger arrived, Francis said to me: "Brother Leo, tomorrow we leave for Rome. Get ready." Well, that was the end of that. We started off early the next morning, allowing ourselves a fortnight of travel because Francis wished to stop in Trevi and Spoleto to visit the friars there, to bring them encouragement. Brother Bernard went with us, at Francis' request. He, too, would rather stay in his hermitage than go to Rome, I think, but Francis liked to have him present where important people gathered because Bernard, born into the nobility, had courtly manners and helped us to behave as we ought.

The farmers along the way were harvesting their grapes, for the summer had come to a speedy end with chilly winds blowing down from the Alps. Sometimes a farmer, recognizing our habits, would offer us a bunch of grapes from the carts making their way to the winepress. And when one asked to be remembered in prayer Francis would stop right there, lest he forget, and ask God's blessing on our benefactor and on his family. He never took lightly anyone's request for prayer, but saw it as a serious duty.

Nor would he miss an opportunity to encourage anyone to be a better Christian. On one occasion, he asked a peasant if he had been to church that day for it was a Sunday. "Not on your life, Brother," he replied. "I don't like to be there with all those hypocrites who sin all week long and then try to look pious on Sunday! I can pray better out here in the open."

"You're probably right, brother," Francis replied, "that they are hypocrites and sinners. So you would fit right in and feel comfortable. We are all hypocrites and sinners. I am, too. Probably the worst one of all. That is what church is for. It is a support group for sinners. It is where we get the encouragement and help to continue on and, hopefully, to change our ways. So don't pretend you're something you're not, brother, and give a better example to your family."

Francis was loving, but he was also truthful and to the point.

When we drew near to Rome, entering the outskirts, I asked, "Where will we stay?"

"Where the Lord provides," returned Francis.

"Oh," I said, thinking I should have known better than to ask. The Lord provided for us a place to stay, all right, and did a fine job of it. A widow, wealthy and charitable, the Lady Jacoba di Settesoli, offered hospitality to those attending the Council. Learning from one of the pope's secretaries the name and address of our hostess, we found our way to her large and magnificent home. Somehow she had heard of Francis, had been longing to meet him, so she was overjoyed to have us as her guests.

"Brother Francis," she said, "I want you to think of this as your home whenever you are in Rome," and she made a sweeping gesture with her hand to indicate the beautiful room, the gilded furniture, the flowering gardens outside the windows. Inside myself I smiled a bit, for such a palace was far from Francis' usual home, a poor hut or a cave.

"Lady Jacoba," he replied, "you are very kind to take into your home three beggars like ourselves. Your generosity will not go unblessed, and I hope that one day we might offer *you* hospitality at St. Mary of the Angels in Assisi."

That is how it happened that Francis and Lady Jacoba became great friends. And indeed she did visit Assisi and Francis did offer her hospitality. In fact he would call her *Brother* Jacoba when she came to the friary and he made her as welcome as any friar. Whenever she came she would arrive laden with gifts, for she was a wealthy woman. She brought candles, cloth for habits, linens for the altar, and always a delicacy that she learned was a favorite with Francis: almond cookies. Everyone knows that years later, when Francis lay dying, he asked that a friar be sent to *Brother* Jacoba to tell her of his death. But before the messenger could leave, a knock sounded at the gate and there stood Lady Jacoba with her servants. She somehow knew that her friend was dying, so she came with gifts: candles for his funeral, a habit for his burial and, yes, some almond cookies.

But I'm getting ahead of my story. The next morning Bernard and I accompanied Francis to the Church of St. John Lateran where the council, already in progress for several days, had been assembled by the pope.

A guard at the door directed us to a secretary where we were assigned to seats within the huge basilica. Francis, as a superior of an Order, was assigned to the section where sat other heads of religious orders and abbots of independent monasteries.

"You may have one person with you," the secretary said, looking disdainfully at our patched habits and bare feet, "as a secretary. Your seats are over there," and he indicated the last row of chairs in the group. Brother Bernard found a seat somewhere behind us with the observers. Here we spent our days for that entire week until the end of the council, listening to the bishops and the pope.

"Excuse me," a voice said. We were on our way out of the basilica at the end of one of the sessions. I recognized him as a monk who sat farther down the row from us. He nodded to me, but he spoke to Francis. "Someone pointed you out as Francis from Assisi. My name is Friar Dominic Guzman of the Order of Preachers."

Even if he had not said his name, his accent would have given him away as a Spaniard. Although not much taller than Francis, who was short, he was more robust. His snapping black eyes and quick gestures indicated a boundless energy ready to erupt into action. I had heard of Dominic Guzman. He was the founder of a group of friars, like ourselves, who were dedicating themselves to preaching, especially to the heretics in

France and northern Italy.

"What Rule of Life will you choose for yourselves, Brother Francis?" he continued. "Now that the council no longer will allow new Rules, we will have to choose the Rule of Saint Benedict or Saint Augustine, perhaps. Which will you and your friars follow?"

"None of those, Brother Dominic," answered Francis, "for we have our own Rule. I and Brother Bernard here came to Rome six years ago and got permission for our way of life from the lord pope. That is the Rule we will continue to follow. I don't want to hear anything of Augustine or Benedict for their ways are not for us. But tell me, Brother Dominic, what have you learned at the council?"

Brother Dominic was known as a very bright fellow, and his followers seemed to be cut of the same cloth because their sermons, at least the ones I had been able to hear, were well prepared and revealed the preachers to be educated men.

"It seems to me, Brother Francis, that we have our work cut out for us. I think the pope commanded us to be here to see the work that needs to be done. There is a great need for an educated clergy, as you know. There are many souls lost to heresies, not through ill will, but the lack of sound teaching of the truth. People need the example of good and prayerful shepherds, so we must be that ourselves and encourage the parish clergy to be holy. Most importantly we must convert and educate the bankers, the politicians, the business people, for they have the influence and power. Don't you think so,

Brother Francis? Will you join me?"

"Oh, dear Brother Dominic," agreed Francis, "you are so right. The people of power and influence need to be converted, need to see that God has blessed them with wealth and talent, yes, but to use those blessings for the poor and unfortunate, not just for their own families. You and your friars will turn many lives to Christ, I know. But as for me and my friars, we are too simple to enter into debates or preach to the rich and powerful. No, our place is with the poor, the uneducated, pointing out what is right and what is wrong. Our calling is to preach more by our lives than with words. Our calling, Brother Dominic, is to live by the work of our hands, supporting ourselves, living the gospel together as brothers among the poor, and to beg only when there is no work for us. Preaching with words is for those who feel called, but preaching by example is for all. You're right, though. Those who preach must be educated, and examined, to be sure they are Catholic. I can see that I have not been cautious enough in sending my own brothers out to preach."

Bernard and I left the two of them talking while we wandered off to look at the wonders of the basilica. It had at one time been the palace of Emperor Constantine but, converted to Christianity, he gave it to the pope at the time; then he and his nobles left Rome for Byzantium, abandoning the western part of the empire to the terrible mercies of the barbarians.

"What are you looking at?" It was Francis.

"Bernard and I were marveling at the beautiful

marble and pillars that popes have taken from pagan temples and old palaces to beautify this church," I replied. "It makes one wonder what the city of Rome might have looked like when Peter and Paul were here."

"Yes, it must have been magnificent. Anyone who puts trust in an earthly city, though, will see it become a ruin one day, like much of Rome nowadays. Brother Dominic and I agreed that even the Church can fall into ruin. It must be renewed, restored, just as we did for San Damiano and St. Mary of the Angels. But the stones for a renewed Church have to be human stones, ourselves, our brothers, people everywhere. Then we will have a really eternal city, one that will last not just for hundreds of years, but forever. We have a lot of work to do! Up to now we have done little or nothing, so let us begin!"

The very next day Francis, Bernard and I left Rome for Assisi to begin again with the missionary work that in only eleven more years would bring Francis, sick and worn out, to his death. It was a work in large part inspired by the council at the Lateran.

CHAPTER

❧ 3 ❧

W E HAD BEEN PREACHING in the Rieti Valley
since mid-October. It had been a glorious
autumn. The wheat crop had been plentiful, the gold-
en fields complementing the russet leaves of the
hedges separating the fields. When we were not
preaching in the towns, we worked in the fields,
alongside the farmers, for our bread. Now November,
the smoky green olive trees on the flanks of the
Apennines were heavy with olives.

When the cold winds began to blow down through
the valley with the promise of an early snow, Francis
said one day: "It is time to give thought to making
ready for Christmas. The gift the newly born Son of
God would appreciate most is a conscience free from
sin and a heart dedicated to him alone. We have been
preaching to others for several months; now let us provide for our own welfare. Let us go join the friars at
Greccio to prepare for Christmas."

There were three of us, Francis, Angelo and me.
When possible, on the road and wider paths, one of us
walked beside Francis instead of single file as we usually did. His eyesight was so poor at that time that he

had difficulty seeing a hole or a stone in the road, so we would guide him around them. And, of course, he could not see well the sunlight on the fields nor the spreading reds and golds of a sunset beyond the distant hills. But he could hear. He would stand still under an oak and listen as Brother Wind, as he called it, sighed in the branches above. "Do you hear?" he would ask. "Brother Wind is lamenting, not the coldness that he brings to us from the north, but the coldness he finds here in so many hearts."

And when a lark would leap up out of a bush alongside the path, giving a startled cry, Francis would smile and say: "Brothers, would that our own hearts would rise so quickly and praise God so beautifully as Sister Lark."

And he could smell. He would sniff the smoke that the wind carried to us from the stubble that farmers were burning in their fields. "Do you smell that, brothers?" he would ask. "Incense that the earth is offering to God." Every creature was a step whereby his mind and heart climbed a staircase to God.

No, he no longer could see well, but he never complained of that nor of the pain that light caused him. Once I asked him: "Francis, don't you regret that you can no longer see well the handiwork of God which you love so much?"

"Leo," he assured me, "I see better now than ever I did before. Before my eyes became ill I used to see only appearances, the outer husk of things. But I am learning now to see the inside, where true beauty lies. Do not feel sorry for me. I am indeed a fortunate man."

"Is that true of people, too, Francis? Can you see what is on the inside of people, too?"

"Sometimes, little lamb. Not all the time, but sometimes I know I am in the presence of a truly holy person. I don't know if 'see' is the proper word for it, maybe 'sense' or 'know.'

"It is like sunlight caught in a many-faceted crystal, brighter than any Venetian craftsman can make. Is it the soul shining out through the person? I suppose it is. Sister Clare is such a person. Brother Bernard another. I tell you, Leo, there is nothing more beautiful on earth, nor above it nor below it, for that matter, not even an angel, I think, more beautiful than a holy person. For what is a holy person, a saint, after all? Someone who loves God perfectly and lets God's love flow through them like sunlight through a stained glass window. That is what we were made for, Leo, little lamb. When a person becomes a complete person, a whole person, we are the greatest work to come from the hand of God."

"How about an evil person, Francis, a person intent on sin?" Angelo asked. "Can you see inside them, too?"

"Yes, sometimes I can. Again, maybe 'see' is not the word to use. It is rare, thank God, but I have sensed, even I could say 'smelled,' evil in a person. It is a frightening and terrifying experience to meet evil for it is the absence of God; it is everything contrary to what you and I long for. But we should not fear such persons, Angelo, for as the Lord says, we should fear God alone and, who knows, maybe God would touch an evil heart through us."

In the distance, atop its high hill, I could see the town of Greccio. I mentioned it to Francis, knowing he could not make it out. "Off there is Greccio," I said. "We should be with the friars in an hour and a half."

"Thank God," he said. "It will be nice to spend Advent in quiet there, preparing for Christmas."

It was more like two hours and a half when we finally arrived at the path leading up the steep slope to the friary above, which seemed to cling to the face of the cliff like a swallow's nest. One of the friars was there on his knees wrestling a large flat stone into place, making a staircase. He got painfully to his feet, a short, stocky friar with strong shoulders and a brush of red hair cut close to his head.

"Welcome, brothers," he said, his bright blue eyes peering at us from under bushy red brows, and he gave each of us a hug. "Where do you come from? Let me take you up to meet the other friars." His hands, grimy and worn from work, indicated the staircase and the friary above us.

Angelo was looking at him closely. "I know you from somewhere," he said. "What's your name? Where do you come from?"

"My name is Brother Placid, and I am originally from Genoa," he said, his eyes sparkling good humoredly in a face that had seen some rough usage. "But in the old days people called me Rufo."

"Rufo! Of course," cried Angelo. "I remember you

now. You were a boxer. I have seen you fight at town fairs. Man, you were a tough fighter! You were not very placid back then!"

"I am afraid you are right, Brother." His craggy face turned red. "I am fighting the Devil now, instead of rough country boys eager to win a few coins from me. Do I know you?"

"No, you probably would not know me. I was a singer of songs, a teller of tales, and I made the rounds of many of the same fairs. Then one day I heard our Father Francis here preach in Urbino, and I decided I would sing for the Lord instead."

"Father Francis," he whispered. He grabbed me by my two arms and looked wide-eyed into my face.

"No, that's Brother Leo," Angelo explained. "This is Francis," and he motioned to Francis who had been standing quietly to one side listening to the conversation, his hood over his head.

Although Placid was short, he was taller than Francis and three times as broad. "Oh, Father Francis," he said, "forgive me for not recognizing you. Ever since I became a friar eight years ago I have wanted to meet you, but never had the chance until now. Can you stay with us here for a while? Please?"

"Brother Placid, we have come for just that reason," said Francis. "To spend Christmas with you and the other friars if we may. And I have wanted to meet you, too. Now help us up this grand staircase you are building."

Placid beamed and started off, leading the way.

"Leo," Francis leaned toward me and whispered, pointing to Placid's broad back. "Did you see the beautiful light in Brother Placid?"

I thought I had, and I nodded.

That Advent, that Christmas, were the most memorable of my life. A time of silence and of peace. The friars there could not have been more hospitable, sharing with us whatever they had, and that was very little. But there was enough. It being a time of fasting, we did not need a great deal.

The third Sunday of Advent a kind shopkeeper from the town of Greccio brought us a rabbit for our meal, it being something of a festive day. As we sat at table, we began talking about Christmas, now only a week and a half away. Francis said: "At Christmas, all of nature should celebrate. Not only we, but everything around us, all of God's creation, injured by Adam's sin, is in mourning and groaning, waiting for the promised coming of God. All of us are waiting to be released. If I were the emperor," he said, "I would decree that all princes and lords in their realms should provide meat and wine for the poor on that most blessed of all days, when the Word of God took on flesh and was born of the Virgin Mary. Not only that, I would decree that grain and fodder should be put out for our brothers and sisters the birds, the deer, for every beast of the forest, for it is the day of promised freedom for them as well."

"Father Francis," Brother Placid spoke up, "if we are to live as Jesus did, for which virtue should we strive the hardest?"

"Which virtue?" echoed Francis softly. "Which virtue makes us most like Christ, dearest Brother Placid?" He slowly got to his feet and, taking his bowl in his hands as though walking in the dark, which in reality he was, for he could not see well, he sat down on the flagstone floor of the dining room, his bowl in his lap. The rest of us instinctively followed his example. We took our bowls, what was left of the roasted rabbit, and some bread, and we sat in a circle there on the floor with Francis.

Looking around at us, tears flowing down his cheeks, he said: "Dearest brothers, it is holy poverty that makes us most like Jesus. This is a great secret, and few there are who know it! Lady Poverty accompanied Mary and Joseph to Bethlehem, showing them to a cave instead of an inn. It was Lady Poverty who welcomed the King of the universe into a wretched stable; it was Poverty who wrapped him in poor rags and placed him in a manger. Poverty was his constant companion throughout his life, and when he hung upon the cross who but Poverty was able to be upon the cross with him? And when he died and was taken from his mother's arms, Poverty laid him in a stranger's tomb.

"Yes, Poverty was our Lord's close companion throughout his life. But since he ascended to heaven, she has wandered the earth searching for someone to love her as Jesus did. No one wants her, everyone drives her away. Until now. Lady Poverty is our dear sister. She must always be sought after and made welcome among us, the Friars Minor, for she will teach us the ways of Christ as long as we honor her."

"Father Francis," sighed Placid, a smile on his battered face that seemed to light up the little dining room, "I wish I could have been there when Jesus was born. Maybe Mary would have let me hold him for a while. Do you think so?"

"Brother Placid, I'm sure she would have," Francis assured him.

The week and a half passed quickly. The night before Christmas Eve it snowed. The world around us was covered with a thin blanket of white that sparkled like jewels in the sun, and occasional flakes drifted down through the freezing but sun-bright air. We had finished our morning prayers and were having a bit of bread and some hot goat's milk in the refectory when Francis said, turning to the superior and shading his eyes with a hand from the sun's bright light coming in through the windows, "Brother Jerome, let us invite the villagers to our midnight Mass tonight."

"Of course, Father Francis," Jerome nodded. "There are a few living nearby who come anyhow, but if we make it known that they are invited, I am sure others will come."

That afternoon Brother Jerome came to me. "Have you seen Francis?" he asked.

"Not lately," I admitted, "but earlier I saw him and Brother Placid going down the steps together. They were laughing and whispering like two unrepentant thieves. Can I help you with..."

"Hold her, hold her, Brother Placid. Be careful she doesn't run off. Push her from behind." Francis' voice carried up to us through the icy air better than he realized.

We looked out a window and there on the stairs below, about halfway up, were Francis and Placid, two sheep and a goat. Francis had a rope around the goat's neck tugging it up the staircase, and farther down Placid was trying to herd the two sheep to follow, but one was reluctant to go any higher.

"Francis," I hollered, "what are you doing? Where did you get those animals?"

Francis turned and peered up at the open window. "Oh, Leo," he said, "it is you? Now it will be no surprise, so come and give us a hand. We are trying to get our brother and sisters up to the chapel. I have explained what we are going to do, but it being Christmas Eve and all, I think they fear the worst about ending up as Christmas dinner instead of being our guests. Come help us." I closed the window, spread my hands at Jerome who was looking at me with questions in his eyes, and went down to them.

"Francis, whose animals are these? What are you doing with them? Why are you taking sheep and a goat to the chapel?" I asked.

"Because I could not find an ox or a donkey that anyone would lend me. And besides, how would Placid and I ever get an ox, or even a donkey, for that matter, up these steps?"

"Oh," I said. "Let me start again. Why are you

bringing *any* animal up these steps to the chapel? Are you sure they're Catholic?"

"Leo, I am not joking. When an ox and a donkey were out of the question, I thought maybe a goat and some sheep would do as well. After all, there were shepherds, so there must have been sheep. And probably goats, too, although maybe not at the manger."

"The manger? Francis, you're bringing these animals into that little chapel up there? How can you ask Brother Jerome to celebrate Mass with a goat in attendance? And maybe the folks you have invited, dressed up in their Christmas finery, would rather not cozy up with a couple of smelly sheep."

"I thought of that, Leo, and I am sure that brother goat and our sisters the sheep will be well-mannered. Since our Lord chose to be born in a stable, I think he will be pleased if we try to imitate that. Besides, I thought *you* might celebrate the Mass tonight, and Jerome will preach."

"Oh," I said.

"Now, will you please go down to the bottom of the steps and bring up the pile of straw that is there? We need it for the manger."

"Oh," I said, squeezed by the goat, the sheep and Brother Placid, and went on down the stairs, managing to step in sheep droppings only once. "It is going to be a different Christmas," I muttered. And of course it was.

It was a cloudless night. For the occasion God liberally sprinkled stars across the heavens and a full moon, reflecting off the snow, made everything a contrast of soft light and deep shadow.

Fifteen or sixteen people came to celebrate midnight Mass with us, some bringing torches to light their way, but it was not really necessary. A few told me they were from the town, Greccio, across the way, but most were from farms down in the valley. One, a florid fellow with work-calloused hands, said his son was with the friars in Rieti, and that he was the owner of the goat and sheep that Francis had borrowed for the night. I thought that he stressed "the night" a bit so that there would be no misunderstanding about how long they were to stay. And although the chapel was small, there was room enough for us all: the altar, the friars, our guests, and in a corner, the goat and two sheep. All of us on our best behavior.

Spontaneously we started to sing Christmas carols. Some few were in Latin, but everyone seemed to know them; others in the Rieti Valley dialect. The tunes were familiar to me, but many of the words were different, so I sang in my own Umbrian dialect and we got along fine.

Three or four children had come with their parents. As the room warmed with the heat of our bodies, the melody of the songs soon had them nodding off to sleep against their parents. One little girl cradled a new doll against her cheek and squirmed under her mother's protective arm.

At the Mass, Francis was the deacon. He incensed the book of the Gospels and began to read the account of the birth of Jesus Christ. "Recite" would be a better word, for he could barely see the words on the page, but that did not matter for he had the text written on his heart.

When he came to Saint Luke's words, "She gave birth to her first-born son and wrapped him in swaddling clothes and laid him in a manger, because there was no room for them in the place where travelers lodged," he paused. We all looked at him, knowing that was not the end of the Gospel reading. Was he feeling alright?

He spoke softly to the little girl: "Little girl, what is your name?"

She blushed and pulled her mother's arm more tightly around her. "Angelina," she whispered.

"Angelina, God's little angel, may I borrow your doll for a moment, to tell better this beautiful story of Christmas? I promise I will return it." She nodded and held it out to him.

Francis took the doll, cradling it in his arms as one would a baby, and moved toward the corner where were the goat, the two sheep and a box into which he had stuffed some straw. "She wrapped him in swaddling clothes," he repeated, "and laid him in a manger."

We all understood then what he was about to do, to reenact for us the splendor of that moment, the awesome poverty of the birth of our Lord. But he stopped again. Brother Placid was standing there; he had been keeping an eye on the goat and the sheep. He had, I saw, tears in his eyes.

"Brother Placid," Francis said to him, "would you care to place our infant Lord on the straw there? There is no room for him, you see, in the inn."

Placid gulped and nodded.

Francis reached out and put in Placid's arms, I swear, *a baby*!

Was it an instant that passed or an eternity? I do not know. But for me, as I look back now many years later, that moment is frozen. Time stopped. We all saw it. Placid was unable to move, his rough hands tenderly holding to his chest the baby. From his face came a glow that seemed to originate somewhere within himself.

Then movement came back to us all. As one we exhaled the breath we had held for I don't know how long. A few of us wiped tears from our eyes. Brother Placid turned and, slowly, tenderly, lay upon the yellow straw—a doll.

Francis returned, a peaceful smile upon his face, to the Gospel Book, and he continued with the account of the birth of Jesus Christ. When he had finished and had kissed the passage he had read, he sat down next to me.

From the corner of my eye I glanced at Jerome. He was supposed to give the sermon now. Jerome did not move. He explained to me later that his legs did not seem to work, and anyhow it did not seem right that he should touch with his words the most beautiful sermon we could ever hope to experience.

After a few moments I heard little Angelina whisper to her mother: "Mama, was that the way it was? Was Jesus even poorer than we are?"

"Yes, sweetest, he was."

In my heart I knew that we had received a special blessing that Christmas. And we had another glimpse of the bond that linked Francis and God. I got to my feet and began with renewed conviction: *"Credo in unum Deum...."*

CHAPTER

4

I T WAS A BLISTERING hot July at St. Mary of the Angels, and the worst, August, was yet to come. Only the mosquitoes seemed to thrive, making sleep difficult.

Francis somehow endured it. Brother Elias, who became general minister on the death of Peter Catanii, had asked him to submit to some cruel cure for his failing eyesight, a treatment which included the searing of his temples with a white hot metal bar. To no avail. His physical condition grew steadily weaker, due both to illness and the hard discipline he had inflicted on his body over the years. But his spirit was not weakened; it seemed to grow stronger as his body faded.

Toward the end of the month he said to me one day, "Leo, before long we will be celebrating the feast of our Lady's Assumption in heaven, and with it will begin the Lent I like to keep before the feast of Saint Michael. Do you know where I would like to observe it this year?"

"Up at the Carceri? That isn't far and won't be hard to get to. Sylvester, Bernard and Rufino would love to have you stay with them."

"No, not the Carceri. I would like to go to La Verna, the mountaintop that Count Orlando gave us. Suppose we start out the first of August? That will give us a fortnight to arrive on time for our Lady's feast. I don't know why, but I feel that the Lord is pulling me there."

"Very well, Francis," I said. "Who will go with us? How about Bernard?"

"No, not Bernard," he replied. "I would hate to pull him away from his meditations. But Sylvester would be glad to go, ask him. And maybe Masseo, too, for he knows where the mountain is and the best way to get there."

Well, as it worked out there were six of us that went. Illuminatus and Tancredius joined us, too, both skillful as masons, for Francis wanted to build a chapel up on the mountain in honor of our Blessed Mother. It would be delightful, I thought, to experience the coolness of the mountain and to sleep at night without being a meal for mosquitoes. I could barely wait to get started.

Three days later, as Francis suggested, on August first, the six of us started off, two hours before the sun had risen from behind Mount Subasio. Even so, farmers were already working in the fields, getting work done before the scorching sun made it impossible.

We traveled by easy stages so as not to tire Francis, and during the hottest part of the day we would rest under a tree. At night we slept in wayside chapels. If these were not well cared for, we always swept them out, leaving them clean and tidy. Such was Francis' devotion for churches. Clare and her Ladies at San Damiano followed his example, sending altar linens that they had made to poor churches.

We had spent two days in Città di Costello because Francis wanted to preach in the square on market day, and also to visit a monastery of nuns who were founded by the Poor Ladies from San Damiano. Going on from there we stopped for the night at a poor little church among some pines on a knoll. The farmer who cared for it unlocked it for us, and his wife cooked some lima beans for us with a bit of bacon and gave us a whole loaf of bread. Lovely people they were!

Eating our supper outside, under a tree, letting an evening breeze circulate through the opened door and windows of the church, freshening it, we watched the sun descend to the hills to the west. Clouds above the horizon began to dress themselves in pink, gold and lavender. The sun was putting on its final display before retiring for the night.

Francis had spent some time alone in the church after Evening Prayer, but now sat cross-legged with us on the grass, his face turned to the sunset. How haggard he looks, I thought. He is so sick, and yet he gives himself little rest. How does he keep going?

Masseo, sitting next to him, said, "Francis, you edify us with the time you spend in prayer, reciting the psalms each day, spending hours in meditation. But what is the best way to pray?"

"I suppose, Masseo, that there are as many ways to pray as there are songs to sing or even words to say. The best way to pray is the one that fits the one who prays, and that might change from moment to moment. One might spend time deep in contemplation, or recite a prayer which someone else composed, or dance about as David did before the Ark.

"Basically all prayer is the relationship between oneself and God. Often I pray by asking a simple question: Who are you, most high God, and who am I, your wretched servant? The more I get to know myself, the more I know God—and the difference between the two.

"And you are right, Masseo, we do spend a lot of time saying prayers, but probably little time praying. Nonetheless, the good God accepts our intention and overlooks our weaknesses. Isn't a great comfort what Saint Paul writes to the Romans: that the Spirit, which we received in baptism, is praying to the Father for us in our hearts because we don't really know how to pray? So do not be concerned, Masseo. Be at peace. Even when we do not realize it we are praying, through the Spirit."

We were all listening intently because Francis, for us, was a living example of prayer.

"Father Francis," Illuminatus asked, "what is the greatest hindrance to prayer?"

"What does our Lord teach us, Illuminatus? Doesn't he say that where one's treasure is there the heart will be? If one's heart is clinging to something other than God, then the heart is not interested in prayer. Each one must examine himself, know himself, to find what that might be. But there are two hindrances to prayer, not just one. The other is hatred. Saint John tells us that God is love. Anyone who has hatred in his heart, who does not forgive, who rejects another, is not choosing God. You recall how often the Lord instructed us to forgive before we can hope to pray: to leave our gifts before the altar and go first to be reconciled with an enemy; to expect forgiveness from him only to the extent we forgive those who trespass against us; to expect no mountain to move until we have forgiven others. That is why we must try to be meek, to have no hatred in our hearts for anyone, if we expect to pray."

We sat there and watched the stars come out. In the pines an owl called; another, a distance away, answered. The world seemed so well ordered: the sun that went down would rise again in the morning; stars twinkled as they had forever; birds lived their lives as God had designed. I felt a great peace within myself, convinced that I, Francis, all of us, were cherished by God. No telling what might lie around the corner of time, but did it really matter?

We arrived at La Verna three days before our Lady's feast, to the surprise of us all because each day had been a bit more difficult, it seemed to us, for Francis. As we stood looking at the mountain before us, Masseo said, "It isn't far to the top, as the bird flies, but for us who have to walk it will be a long and steep climb. Do you feel up to it, Francis?"

"The Lord knows that we have climbed mountains far more steep than this one," Francis replied. "Isn't that right, Leo?"

"That is true," I agreed, "but we were younger and our legs stronger. Why spend all your energy climbing the mountain, Francis, and then have none left when you get to the top? We just passed a farm not a half-mile back and I noticed the farmer had a mule. Let us ask him if he would, for the love of God, give you a ride to the top? What do you say?"

"I hate to admit it, Leo, but I have to agree that I am about worn out. If you say so, then go and ask him."

"Sylvester," I asked, "will you please go back and ask that farmer to help us? Be sure that you ask him to do it for the love of God." And as Sylvester went off I whispered that he should also tell the farmer that it was Francis of Assisi who needed his help. Although they might never have laid eyes on him, many people knew of him.

Before long Sylvester was back and with him a bright-eyed young man of about eighteen riding a gray, tired-looking mule. He jumped off the mule when Sylvester pointed to Francis and said, "Francis, this is Feruccio. His father has sent him with the mule to help us up the mountain."

"Thank you, Feruccio. God will bless you for your kindness," said Francis, giving him a pat on the arm. "Are you and your mule ready to go?"

"Yes, sir. I have been up there often to look for mushrooms, so I know a good path. Let me help you up on Lightning and we will get started."

"Lightning?" I asked. And I thought Francis was

looking at the mule with wary interest.

"Well, Lightning may have lost most of her spark because she is as old as I am. But she will be honored to give you a ride, sir," he said to Francis. "Here put your foot in my hands."

Together we helped Francis up on Lightning. What a difference, I thought, between the handsome young knight in full armor who had gone off on a beautiful charger to do battle against Perugia and this sick man in a ragged habit astride a worn-out mule. And the difference was far more than appearances.

"Let us go, then," Francis smiled, "and give Feruccio here time to get back home before dark."

Even on a cool autumn day one would break into a sweat laboring up Mount La Verna. There is always the possibility of a scorpion in the shade of a rock where you would put your foot, or maybe a viper, although snakes usually come out at night and avoid humans. It was a hard climb, not without dangers, and the sun made it a torture, as we carefully, slowly, struggled upward.

Before we were a quarter of the way along the path Feruccio, leading the mule, turned and said to us, "We will stop here for a moment and drink a little water." I looked around for the spring, saw none, and looked back at Feruccio.

"You didn't bring a jug of water with you? What are you going to do for water?" The implication, of course, was that we were thoughtless.

"There is water up there," Masseo said. "A cistern

of rain water."

Feruccio shook his head, turned and continued on up the path leading Lightning.

Maybe it was his suggestion, but I was beginning to become very thirsty, too. I was soaked with sweat from the climb in the hot sun.

Suddenly Feruccio turned and slumped in the middle of the path. "I can go no farther," he wailed. "I am dying of thirst. You must be crazy to try to climb this mountain on a hot day like this without any water. And look at Lightning! She will die if she doesn't get some water."

I looked at the mule. To be sure, she was a forlorn specimen of a mule, but she did not seem to be much worse than when we started.

"Feruccio, Feruccio," said Francis, "if you look behind that juniper bush yonder you will find a little spring. You can quench your thirst there, and we will all take a little rest from the climb. Lightning, too, I am sure, would appreciate it if I got out of the saddle for a while."

"There is no spring there," answered Feruccio. "I have been up this path, all over this mountain plenty of times. There are no springs up here. Anyhow, how would you know? You've never been here before!"

"Just the same, Feruccio, go look. Get up and see if what I say is true."

Feruccio got to his feet and walked about thirty feet to look behind the large juniper bush that Francis had pointed out.

"You are right," he shouted. "There *is* a spring here! Come on! Bring Lightning!"

So we all went to look and there (why was I not surprised?) was a spring. It issued from a split in the side of the mountain, ran along the mountainside for about ten feet, forming a pool, and disappeared down a crack.

Feruccio was lying on his stomach, his face in the pool of water. "It is like ice water, and it tastes so good," he said, raising his head and shaking water from his curly hair. "I cannot believe that I never found it before. Nor that you knew about it, sir. Someone told you about it, right?"

"Yes," Francis agreed, "someone told me about it."

We each drank from the stream, Lightning, too, and even washed our feet there when we had drunk our fill. Francis would not hear of sitting for a while in the shade of an oak that grew there. "We will rest when we get to the top," he said. "Feruccio will have to leave with Lightning so as to get home before dark."

The top of La Verna is a place of dense woods, tumbled boulders and clefts in the rock that separate it into islands of solitude. Tall oaks and a few pines crowded upon each other reaching upward toward the sun and their roots searching the thin soil below for nourishment. Francis fell in love with the place at once, calling it a holy mountain, saying it must have been shaken by the earthquake at the moment of Christ's death.

As soon as Feruccio started back down the mountain with Lightning, carrying with him our thanks and assurances of our prayers for him and his family, we began work, weaving branches together to form some huts for ourselves to ward off the night breezes and the dew. Tomorrow we would mark off the dimensions of our chapel in honor of Saint Mary and begin to build.

The following weeks were wonderful indeed. There was a place where the mountain thrust a spur maybe eighty feet above us and at the bottom of it were several overhangs, like caves, that we easily enclosed with stone, making dwellings for ourselves. And we sometimes needed them during those weeks for violent storms would descend upon the mountain with little warning. Lightning on several occasions struck some trees, scattering splinters in every direction and filling the air with an acrid smell. The earth would shake as we huddled there in our caves, grateful to be secure from the wind and rain.

Francis, however, was not with us. He had chosen one of those islands of boulders and oaks where, he told us, he would spend his time in prayer. We built for him a cell, walling up much of an opening under a huge boulder that lay tumbled against another. Most of his time, though, I suspected, was spent out in the open, praying, for he delighted in the uncultivated world of nature, sometimes confiding to us the lessons that an insect, a plant, taught him.

There was the trunk of a fallen tree that lay across the crevice separating his island from where we were building the chapel. He had left firm instructions that I was the only one to come over to him and that before doing so I should say: "Oh Lord, open my lips," the beginning verse for Matins. If he replied: "And my mouth will proclaim your praise," then I was to cross over on the fallen log and we would recite Matins together. But if he did not respond, I was to come no closer. If he needed bread or water he would tell me, he said, to bring that the next day.

Everything went well enough. We were all keeping the same Lent, along with Francis, which meant fasting and trying to put more time at prayer. We had managed to lay the foundation for the chapel and had raised the walls to shoulder height before a month was out. Count Orlando, somehow hearing that we were there, had sent a yoke of oxen and several men to help us for a few days, so we soon had a pile of stones ready at hand, and the promise of more help when we got to the roof. The work, the prayer, filled our days.

By the first week of September it was noticeably cooler up there on the mountain. Here and there a leaf changed color. Autumn, winter, too, would come much sooner to La Verna than to Assisi. Francis' prayer must be more intense, I thought, at the end of that first week. Now and then he had not responded to me in the morning so, following his directions, I had returned to our own area. He had taken very little bread the whole time, and he had a jar of water, but at the end of that week he stopped responding to me at all. And he asked for no food, of course. After several days of no reply to my "Oh Lord, open my lips," I became truly concerned. I mentioned it to the others.

"Leo, don't worry about it," Masseo said. "You

know how he can go forty days at a time on next to nothing to eat. He gave you instructions, follow them."

"If it were I, Leo," joined Sylvester, "I would go over there to see what is going on. You know better than we how sick he has been. He could be lying helpless over there. You have an obligation to look out for him."

So I was divided.

Finally, I could stand it no longer. We were almost midway through September. I shall never forget the day if I live to be two hundred. The fourteenth, it was. All night long I had been more awake than asleep, listening for any sound that might come from where Francis was. With every cry of an owl my heart jumped thinking it was Francis calling to me for help. With every fall of a dead branch from the trees above my anxious ears heard the body of Francis fall into one of the crevices. I could hardly wait for dawn because I had determined what I would do. Chancing Francis' displeasure, I had to assure myself that he was well.

What I am going to relate now, the bare facts of it, is well enough known now by nearly everyone. But because I and I alone was present as a witness, it is right, I think, that I set down what I saw happen that day on Mount La Verna so many years ago.

There had been a bit of frost during the night. The day, when the sun came up, was one of those early autumn days, crystal clear and brisk. Sound was amplified, so that the quarreling crows seemed closer than they were, and in the woods around the squirrels chattered to each other as they ran through leaves already fallen from the trees.

I armed myself with some bread, a jar of fresh water and, of course, the Breviary, and picked my way across the fallen log to Francis' place of seclusion. "Oh Lord," I called hopefully, "open my lips." The words went out through the trees, bounced among the boulders and came back to me unanswered.

"Oh Lord, open my lips," I cried again, louder. Nothing. Behind me, muffled by the undergrowth, I could hear the others at work shaping stones for the chapel walls. Ahead of me I heard no sound. But wait! Was that a moan? Was Francis hurt? Was he sick? I put on the ground the jar, the bread, the Breviary, and cautiously, not to make a sound, went in the direction of that moan.

Francis was standing in a small clearing outside the shelter we had made for him. His back was to me so I could not see his face, but his figure appeared more frail than ever under the patched habit that the morning wind stirred around his legs. He seemed to have heard something or noticed something in the sky, for he was looking, not toward the sun which had come over the mountain behind him, but out over the valley beneath the clearing in which he was standing. His eyesight was not good. What could he be looking at? Perhaps he was listening to something I could not hear, or he sensed something that was beyond me. Whatever it was, he was absorbed and unmindful of my presence or of anything around him.

And then I saw what Francis saw or sensed. At first I thought it to be a hawk or an eagle, for often I had seen them riding the morning breezes that rose from the valley below as they studied the ground for an unlucky squirrel or hare. But it did not move as a bird does, drifting with the wind. It was moving, and I could see wings, yet it was approaching straight on, directly toward us, becoming clearer as it came.

It came nearer, and the closer it came, it was larger. Now I could see that it was not a bird, but a cross, with wings. Rather it was the figure of a man, but on a cross; and the figure—I hesitate to call it a man for although it looked like a man's body, I don't know if it was a man. It flew. It had wings. Six. Two of the wings were folded about the figure's body. Two were upright, extended over the figure's head, and with two wings it flew.

The figure—what shall I call it? A seraph? It approached Francis, who was standing enrapt, his back to me, looking at it. Maybe twenty feet away from Francis it stopped, hovering, a bit above him. The figure of a man was life size. I could not tell, but Francis seemed to be completely absorbed in what he saw. If anything was spoken, I do not know for I heard not a sound; but after a moment Francis slowly spread his arms in the same way the seraph's arms were extended against the cross. With his whole body stretching itself forward toward the seraph, he threw his head back and he screamed, the scream of a man in great pain, a scream that went out over the valley and cut through my heart. For another moment he stood there, as though nailed to a cross of his own, and then slowly he lowered his arms, his knees buckled and he crumpled to the ground. The seraph withdrew a bit, slowly, and then, moving more quickly, sped upward and was gone from sight.

What should I do? Was Francis dead? Was he hurt in some terrible way? I knew that I had witnessed something that I had no right to see. I had intruded into an encounter so personal, so intimate, that I was ashamed for being there. And I was afraid, for what I had witnessed was beyond the realm of my experience. Then, with a sob, a moan like I had heard before, Francis seemed to gather his strength and he sat up. Slowly I backed away; without a sound I returned to the fallen tree that bridged the crevice, retrieved the Breviary and bread and the jug of water, and went back to where the rest were laboring at the chapel walls. My hands were trembling, my legs felt weak beneath me.

The others were hard at work. When asked if I had seen Francis and how he was, I merely nodded and said he seemed fine. My reticence they seemed to take as an indication that indeed Francis was well and my concern was for nothing, so they did not pursue it.

The next morning, at the proper time, I once again crossed the log with bread, water and Breviary and shouted out: "Oh Lord, open my lips." Somewhat to my surprise I heard a muffled "And my mouth will declare your praise," so I proceeded to Francis' shelter. At first I failed to see him. But then I noticed that he was sitting, cross-legged, inside, out of the growing light of morning.

"Good morning, Francis," I said. "Are you all right?"

"Good morning, Leo," he said, not answering my question. "This morning why don't you read the Office and I'll listen."

Ordinarily we would sit side by side, passing the Breviary back and forth as we recited the psalms together. "You will see better there where you are, and I can hear you well enough." For some reason he doesn't want to sit out here with me, I thought. Maybe the light is giving his eyes more pain than usual.

"Very well, Francis," I agreed, sitting down, and I began to recite slowly and clearly, so he could hear, the psalms for the day. When we had finished, he thanked me, and I told him I had brought water and some bread in case he needed it.

"Thank you, Leo. You are a good friend. For many years now you have been so faithful, so helpful. My right hand, as it were. Now I need your help even more." His voice was weak, maybe from his fast, I thought.

"Francis, I have been glad to be of help in whatever way I can. What is it you need? Are your eyes bothering you more today? Do you want me to fetch something, is that it?"

"No, Leo. Do you recall how we used to go to the caves, years ago, before San Damiano, and spend time praying?"

"Of course," I said. "That's not so long ago."

"And how we did not tell each other what the Lord had said to us in prayer?"

"That is true." Francis had always, since I had known him, been very closed-mouthed about any favors he received from God. Even years later, after long periods of prayer in seclusion, he would say, more to himself than to anyone else, "My secrets are mine. They are for me." As though he feared he might lose any graces God had given him if he talked about his prayer to another.

"I need your help, Leo. But I want you to promise me that you will not tell another person, during my lifetime, what I tell you now. Will you promise me that?"

"Of course, Francis. You know I do not tell others what you tell me."

"I know, Leo, but I want to impress this on you."

"Very well."

"Come over here, then, Leo, by the door." He inched himself, painfully, I thought, out of the interior shadows to the doorway of his shelter.

"Yesterday," he said, looking at me intently as I squatted on the ground near him, "while I was praying, the Lord touched me."

"Touched you?" I looked at his anguished face. The memory of yesterday overflowed from his eyes and flowed as tears down his cheeks.

"Look," he whispered. He pulled the hem of his habit away from his feet and held out his hands toward me, his palms toward each other.

I caught my breath. In the palms of his hands were angry-looking wounds. In the middle of each wound was what appeared to be the head of a nail, and around it open bloody flesh. The nails, which appeared to be of cartilage, protruded from the back of his hands, bent back. On the instep of each foot, the same, the head of a nail imbedded in a bloody wound, and the nail sticking out on the bottom of his feet, bent back.

"Oh, Francis," I cried. And I wept. His pain was intense, I knew. I almost said "I am so sorry," but that was not what I should say. I did not know what to say. I said nothing.

He smiled wanly. "I asked Jesus to let me know what he suffered for my sins," he confided. "He suffered a lot, Leo.

"Now," he continued, "remember your promise. I do not want anyone to know about this, not even the other friars." His voice was so low and weak that I had difficulty hearing him.

"But Francis," I said, "it is going to be evident that something has happened. For one thing, how are you going to walk? You will need help. And people will see your hands."

"We will bandage my hands. And my feet, too. And maybe we can sew some extra cloth to the sleeves to make them longer, and to the bottom of the habit, too. You know what will happen, Leo, if people think I have the wounds of Christ. They will forget about Jesus' suffering and come to look at me. No, this is my secret."

"Sylvester and the others are going to realize that

something has happened to you," I objected. "You will have to tell them something!"

"Leo," he replied, "you be the one to help me. I will eat by myself from now on, and I will keep bandages on my hands and feet so nobody will see anything. From now on I will travel by mule instead of walking. People will think I am not well, which is true enough. We just will not say anything about this. Do you agree?"

"All right, Francis, if that is the way you want it."

That was the way we did it. It was still two weeks until the feast of Saint Michael, when Francis would end his Lent, time for him to recover a bit from what happened. Our routine did not change. In the morning I would go to the log, cross over and holler out the verse we had agreed on. Sometimes he would not reply, as he had not done before, so I would leave him to his private prayers. Most mornings, though, he would answer me, "And my mouth will declare your praise," and I would go to where he sat in the doorway of his shelter.

The day before the feast of Saint Michael I said to him, "Francis, tomorrow's feast will mark the end of your forty days of prayer. What are your plans? The weather is changing, as you've noticed. It might be better for you and all of us to leave here before the cold sets in."

"How far along is the chapel?" he asked. "I feel bad that all of the work has been left to you and the others."

"Count Orlando's men came at the beginning of the week. The beams and ribs are up. We even covered over the roof with planks to keep the snow out. They suggested that we make the roof steeper than usual for the snow gets deep and heavy up here. For now we have done all we can, Francis, until warm weather returns."

"Very well, Leo, let us celebrate the feast tomorrow, and then on the first of October begin our return to Assisi. Even though it is downhill, I think I might need the help of Feruccio and Lightning to get down the mountain. Would you ask Sylvester to go down to that good farmer and ask him, for the love of God, to send us once again his son and his mule?"

Two days later, leaning on me, and with the help of a stick, Francis made it over to where the chapel and our shelters were. I had sewed some cloth to the ends of his sleeves and to the hem of his habit, so he kept his bandaged feet and hands from sight. But he could not hide the pain in his face with each step he took nor the fact that he was even more thin and frail. I could see the concern on the faces of the other friars as they looked at him, but no one asked a question.

Already the trees were at their peak of color, seeming to tint the sunlight as it filtered through red and yellow leaves. The air was brisk, even though the sun was bright overhead. Francis sat on one of the large stones Count Orlando's men had dragged there for the building and he shivered a bit under the cape that he pulled more tightly around himself.

We heard the snap of twigs and the whisper of feet through dry leaves before Feruccio, leading Lightning, appeared around the bend in the trail that came up from the valley. "Good morning, brothers," he called. "Here we are, at your service, Lightning and me. Say, what a nice church! You did a lot of work while you were up here."

"Good morning, Feruccio," I said. "Thanks for coming up here with your mule. We truly appreciate it. Francis, here is your steed."

Francis seemed to be lost in his thoughts, the hood pulled over his head. But at the mention of his name he raised his head and, peering from under the hood, smiled at Feruccio. "God bless you, Feruccio, for helping this poor beggar. The older I get, it is harder for me to go up and down mountains."

He got slowly and stiffly to his feet. "Leo," he said softly to me, "perhaps you and Sylvester can help me to get up on Lightning."

I motioned to Sylvester to help me and to Feruccio to bring the mule closer. We had to lift him up on the mule for he was unable to help himself. Sylvester, who was on Francis' right side, put his hand under Francis' arm to help him up, but his hand must have touched Francis in the rib area. He winced noticeably and gasped. Both Sylvester and I noticed it, and we looked at each other. Could it be, I wondered, that Francis also had a wound in his side, which he had kept hidden from me, as Jesus had a wound from the soldier's lance? That would explain why he moved so stiffly.

Seated on the mule his feet hung below the hem of his habit, but I had wrapped them with cloth, as though to ward off the cold, thus hiding the bandages.

Everyone could see his wrapped feet, but no one said a word. And so we started off down the path, Feruccio leading the mule and the rest of us following.

Looking back at Francis, Feruccio said, "I searched for that spring on the way up here this morning, sir, but it was not where I thought it was. Maybe you could show it to me again, if you remember."

"Maybe, Feruccio," Francis replied. And then, more to himself than to anyone I heard him say: "Goodbye, mountain of peace, mountain of grace."

"Francis, we can return in the spring, when the weather permits," I said.

"I think not, little lamb of God," he replied. "I think not."

CHAPTER
❧5❧

M AYBE IT WAS THE ATTRACTION of returning to its stall, maybe the crispness of the October day, but Lightning set a fast pace for us going down the mountain that morning. There was no need to stop for a rest, nor did Feruccio mention the spring Francis had discovered for him on the way up.

I have to admit that I was worried. Although Francis seemed to be doing well enough despite a few missteps by the mule on the steep path that must have jarred him and hurt his side, what would we do when we reached the bottom and he had to dismount? He certainly was incapable of walking. How would we get him back to Assisi? Masseo supplied an answer to my concern.

He and I were bringing up the rear of our procession. Pulling me by my sleeve, he said to me quietly, "Leo, I've been watching Francis. He is evidently not well, and he must be weak if he would consent to ride a mule. I do not want to pry into why he is wearing those bandages on his feet nor why he seems to be in pain. It seems foolish to me to expect that he walk all the way back to Assisi. What if we take him to Count

Orlando's castle? It is only a short distance. And there maybe we can persuade the Count to send Francis back home on a horse. What do you think?"

That is what we did. The Count was more than gracious. Not only did he lend us a horse, he sent several of his knights with us as companions. And Francis, who made it a point never to ride horseback nor allow his friars to do so, because horses were a mark of wealth and power, nonetheless acquiesced and allowed himself to be put upon a gentle mare. That in itself was for all of us an indication of the pain he was suffering and of his weakened condition.

Our return journey brought us to the city of Arezzo. The sun that day shone brightly all around us bathing us in its warmth. But about the city there seemed to be a drape of darkness that enveloped it like a mist rising from the city itself. On the crest of a hill we had paused to look at the odd appearance of the city when one of the knights accompanying us said, "Brother Francis, it will be best if we not enter Arezzo to look for a place to stay tonight. Even if we have to sleep under the stars we will be better off, for these days it is a dangerous place. The leading families are fighting each other, making it unsafe for citizens and strangers alike."

We continued on. The road lay close to the walls of the city and brought us not far from the main gate before continuing on to the south towards home. Francis, who had difficulty seeing and had his hood pulled over his head because of the sun's glare, motioned for all of us to stop.

"Do you smell that?" he asked of no one in particular.

There was a breeze blowing in our direction out of the gate, but I had not noticed anything unusual over the bad odor coming from any populated area.

"Arezzo reeks of violence, of hatred and jealousy," he continued. "There are more devils making their home here than people. Sylvester, drive them out. Send them back to hell!"

Sylvester, who had been standing next to the horse Francis was mounted on, looked over at me with a dismay on his face and, pointing his thumb at his chest he mouthed the word, "Me?"

"Go ahead, Sylvester," Francis encouraged him. "Go over to the gate there and draw down from heaven your priestly blessing upon this wretched town. Tell all the devils here that they must depart in the name of Jesus and consign them to hell where they belong. Do not be afraid and do not doubt that your blessing can do it. Now go. Bring God's peace to the unfortunate people who are captive here."

Sylvester gritted his teeth and marched off toward the gate that stood open about fifty feet from us. He looked back at us to see if we were indeed waiting for him.

"Dear Father in Heaven," Francis prayed, "listen to the prayer of your humble servant and priest Sylvester. Grant power to his blessing, the power that comes from the merits of your Son and our Brother Jesus who overcame the curse of sin and freed us from the chains the devil would put upon us. Free Arezzo from the mischief and the control of the great liar."

We could not hear what Sylvester shouted, what prayer he hurtled through the open gate and through the streets of the city, but we saw him raise his arm and watched him make a large sign of the cross. When he had done so he stood there with his back to us for a moment. Then we saw him back up a few paces before he turned and started to run back down the road toward us. Then I heard it. It started like a murmur, as of a disturbed hive of bees, somewhere within the city. The sound grew into a roar like that of an avalanche when dislodged snow roars down the slope of a mountain, and exploded out of the city gate knocking Sylvester flat on his face in the road. Up into the air over the city hurtled myriads of demons as debris is thrown from Mount Vesuvius. A veritable eruption of devils. We could see them with our astonished eyes.

"Go back to hell!" Francis shouted. "In the name of Jesus, our Savior, leave this city in peace!" The words seemed to hang over the city in the ensuing silence like a protective hand which brushed away the gloom and shadows, allowing the sunlight to bathe the walls, the tiled roofs of the old city to gleam gold and pink in the afternoon. "Come, Sylvester, come here for a well-deserved rest," he called.

"Leo," he said to me. "Take me over to the side of the road here and help me down. Then all of you go into town to get some food. Sylvester and I will wait for you here. And bring a bit of wine back with you," he called after us. "It is only right to celebrate what the Lord has done today through Sylvester." Sylvester still looked a bit dazed, not sure that he should celebrate for Arezzo or for his own escape. But he sat alongside Francis in the grass to await our return.

In less than an hour we were all back, and we gathered around Francis. We were laughing and congratulating each other on what we had begged from, as Francis always put it, "the table of the Lord." Illuminatus had half a loaf of bread and a length of sausage. Tancredius proudly displayed a roasted pigeon. Masseo, the youngest and most vivacious of the group, contributed half a meat pie, several pieces of bread and some goat cheese that might have seen better days. And I, I was glad to contribute a flask of wine and several cooked artichokes that a pious widow had pressed upon me. We were reveling in the goodness of God when we became aware of the knights who had also gone into town. They were standing a bit shyly around us, looking at the results of our begging.

"What is the matter?" asked Francis. "Aren't you going to eat?"

"We were unable to buy any food there in town," one of them complained. "None of the citizens would sell us anything. I think they are still wary of anyone who is a stranger or has a weapon."

"And with good reason," commented Francis. "But look, what your flies cannot do for you"—he often called money "flies," as something dirty—"the love of God will. Go back into the city and do as we did: beg the people to share their food with you for the love of God. You will see that they will give you more than enough to eat, as they have done for us."

So the knights went back into the city and, swallowing their pride, they did as Francis told them: They begged for food. And soon, even more elated than we, they were back with enough food for all of them to eat to join us on the grass among some olive trees by the side of the road. Does anyone realize, I wondered, what marvelous riches of holiness lay hidden under the patched habit of this little man from Assisi? Evidently he was coming to the end of his life. How would we go on without him? I looked at him as he leaned back against the trunk of an olive tree, and wondered if these knights, even if we who followed him, appreciated his closeness to God. Even now, years later, I look back on the years spent with Francis as time spent in the presence of God.

The remainder of the journey back to St. Mary of the Angels was not an easy one, but with the assistance of the knights and with no haste we finally arrived. The friars were overjoyed to have Francis back with them, and he was able to guard his condition from everyone, even greatly from me, who took care of his needs. But of course rumors would circulate and people wondered, but I was sworn to secrecy and told no one what I had seen there on Mount Alverna nor what I knew of the wounds he bore in his feet, his hands and side. So people were content. Except one. Sister Clare. She wanted to see Francis, to see for herself that he was all right. At every opportunity she would send word to him that she longed to see him, but Francis was reluctant to go to San Damiano to visit the sisters, for fear, as he said, that they rely upon him for comfort and direction instead of upon the Lord.

Finally, because of her evident desire to see him and her perseverance in her request, Francis instructed me to tell Sister Clare that he would meet with her. Not at San Damiano, however, but that she should join him one day, a Wednesday, at midday in an olive grove that belonged to his father, down the hill from her monastery, and they would have a bite to eat together. So on that day Francis asked me to accompany him, and we started off through the fields, a lovely day in mid-November. The olives still had not been gathered and they hung, dark and fat with oil on the branches.

There, under one of the trees, sat Sister Clare and another nun. She had brought with her as a companion her mother, Ortolana, who had joined the monastery after the death of her husband, Clare's father. It had been years since I had seen Ortolana, but I recognized her at once from the times I would see her in the market on Saturdays or in the cathedral where she attended Mass with her family. They had spread a cloth on the ground and on it were some bread, a jug of water, some apples and figs. A simple meal, but I suppose it was a feast for them who never ate meat and fasted most of the year. After a hug from Clare and a motherly peck on the cheek from Ortolana we sat down around the cloth, and Clare asked Francis if he would bless the food we were about to share.

A tinkling choir of Assisi's bells from the cathedral, San Rufino, from the churches of St. George and San Masseo, from the cloisters of nuns, spread out over the valley and the slope of Mount Subasio the noontime Angelus. Francis listened a moment and lifted his nearly sightless eyes toward the city. "Dear God, our loving Father," he prayed, "as you call us now to prayer in honor of our Blessed Lady, warm our cold hearts as you warmed this world of ours through the birth of Jesus whom you desired to give us through her. We offer up our gratitude for your generous gift of life and the food with which we sustain it. Nourish our bodies with this food and our souls with your grace that we might serve you faithfully and joyfully. Amen."

"Amen," we all said.

Sunlight filtered through the gray-green leaves above us, dappling the cloth and the food.

Sister Clare was studying the face of Francis who sat cross-legged, his hands hidden by his sleeves. "You look tired," she observed. "How are you feeling?"

"Not well," he admitted. "Brother Body has always complained of the penance he has had to do, and now he insists that I give him better care or he will not be able any longer to do even the smallest tasks. So I have apologized for the rough treatment he has had to suffer, but even so I have to control him lest he think he is my master. Illness is its own blessing, however, because it introduces us and prepares us for Sister Death. It is a reminder that we are very fragile.

"But we did not come here to talk about illness and death, did we Clare? Let us talk about life and the Source of all life."

As he was speaking, a ladybug lit on the bridge of his nose. His vision was not good enough to see what it was, and he was always careful to give no harm to any living creature so instead of brushing it off he turned to me. "Leo, what is this visitor on my nose?"

"A ladybug," I replied.

He gently put a finger up to the insect which obligingly crawled upon it. Holding his finger out to us with the ladybug, he said, "Sister Ladybug here perhaps, if she could speak, could tell us more of the goodness, the magnificence of God, than any theologian. Look, Clare, look Sister Ortolana, how small and delicate, how carefully made. God provides for her even better than he does for you and me for we have to harvest the wheat and mill the flour and make the bread, but God prepares the table for her. And does she refuse to honor God? No, just by going about her life she is praising her Creator. There is so much we can learn from our lesser brothers and sisters in creation if we had the humility to let them teach us."

The time slipped away from us that afternoon; we were so caught up in the enthusiasm of Francis. We talked about the love of God for us, we praised him for his goodness and we lamented our lack of fervor. Before we knew it the bell at San Damiano was announcing Vespers and still we had eaten nothing.

"Clare," said Francis, "your sisters are calling you.

And we must go."

"Francis, Leo, thank you for the lovely afternoon." Sister Ortolana smiled her agreement.

"You must come and stay with us," she said, looking at Francis with concern. "The sisters and I would be glad of the opportunity to care for you in your illness. We could have a little house built for you outside the wall so that you would be close by and we could nurse you back to health. Please say you'll come."

"Thank you, Clare, I will. But not yet. I still have the strength in me to preach, so I must do that for as long as I can. I will go to Foligno and Perugia and the other cities here in Umbria; then I will come to you.

So Francis had himself carried by litter to the town and villages around, no longer able to walk because of the wounds in his feet, sometimes more dead than alive, I think, to encourage others to carry the cross of Christ as they could see that he was doing. When one of us would try to restrain him, he would say, "Brothers, we must begin to serve the Lord our God. Up to now we have done very little."

It was just about a year later that Francis, I and Bruno, who had been the chaplain to the king of Naples, were in Spello preaching in the cathedral. How Francis was able to continue to preach that year before he died, I do not know. More by his presence and appearance he turned people's hearts to God, I am sure, for his voice was weak. His sermons were usually simple in content, urging repentance from sin and assuring everyone of God's infinite love.

"Leo, little lamb of God," he said to me one evening after Bruno and I had heard the confessions of several people. "Do you recall what Sister Clare said when we ate with her and her mother after our return from Mount Alverna, that she would have a little house put up outside the wall of their garden and that she and the sisters would nurse me back to health?"

"Yes, I remember. It was about a year and a half ago, at the olive harvest. Why?"

"It is time now, Leo. I am not able to do any more. Brother Body has done all he can do. He needs to rest."

He was so weak that we had to arrange for a litter to carry Francis from Spello to San Damiano. It had rained during the night. The smell of the wet earth drying in the sun was a perfume that enveloped us.

I knew that Francis was not giving in or giving up. I understood that he realized the reality of his condition. He was no longer able to see. In fact sunlight caused him great discomfort. He would often be seized by terrible coughing, even at times spitting up blood from his thin chest. His legs and feet were swollen from dropsy, and his body was weak from years of fasting. There was never a complaint, however, and although he needed medical attention he would allow no one to examine him. I was the only person he allowed to help him and even I, although he had sworn me to secrecy, never saw his wounds again since that day on Mount Alverna. It was only out of obedience to Brother Elias that he allowed a doctor to treat his blindness, a useless torture of searing his temples with a white-hot metal bar. As he used to say, his secrets were his own.

One day, after midday prayers were finished, he confided in me, "Leo, do you know what I would like to do when I feel better?" I quickly reviewed in my mind the things that he had done since he had started to walk in the footsteps of Jesus. He had first cared for lepers for a bit in Gubbio, then he had rebuilt churches, he had gone about preaching, he had been a missionary in the Holy Land and lived the life of a hermit.

"No," I replied, "what would you like to do?"

"I believe I would like to care for lepers," he said. When he said that it struck me that Francis had gone full circle, ending up wanting to do what he had first done: care for the most unfortunate of all, lepers. It dawned on me then that what Francis did, his ministry, was not the important ingredient of his life, giving it direction. His vocation was to imitate Jesus, to live the gospel, and he had done that. While living the gospel he had busied himself in various activities and ministries. The marks that he now bore on his body were an acknowledgment of who he was and not of what he had done.

The sisters did what they could to make Francis comfortable, but there was little they could do other than make sure he ate food that agreed with his stomach. The little hut became ever more hot as summer grew through July and August. Because of the torment that sunlight caused him, Francis had to stay within the darkness of the hut during the day, venturing out only at night. Because of the heat and his ailments the poor man had little rest, even to the extent that sometimes mice would get into the hut and run across his face and body while he was trying to sleep. But never did he complain. In fact, he maintained a joyful spirit, somewhat to the dismay, I fear, of some of the brothers. Francis, always a lover of songs, especially those in French, would sing some ditty that he remembered from his youth and ask me and the other friars who happened to be there to join with him. On one occasion, when Brother Elias, the General Minister of the Order, happened to be there and he heard Francis singing, he suggested that he not do so because he might disedify the people.

"Dearest Brother Elias," replied Francis, "if you command me to forego singing, I shall do so, but I must tell you that in my heart I will still be singing, for it is only right that I rejoice in the sufferings I am able to bear for our Lord, as he bore his sufferings for us. Sadness and sorrow are a sign of weak faith, brother, and do not become a Friar Minor." So Elias let the matter drop and we continued to sing.

One of the songs that Francis enjoyed, especially when someone could accompany him on the lute or the violin, was the song that he himself had composed and called "The Song of the Creatures." It was at that time, living in the little house close to the wall of San Damiano, that he added the last two stanzas to his song. It happened in this way:

One evening, the sun having set beyond the hills to the west, Francis and I were sitting outside, our backs against the house. Because he was confined there I was telling him the latest news about the brothers and the area. He knew all the families for miles around on the farms and most of the people in the city as well. He was always keenly interested in who was sick, who was undergoing difficulties, and so on. So I mentioned that the bishop of Assisi and the mayor were once again in conflict. In those days when the commune was trying to maintain its independence from Perugia and the emperor, it also did not want to become too indebted to the pope, so it was not difficult to find something to disagree about. Anyhow, the two had quarreled, each naming the other a meddler and a tyrant, and were not speaking. He, Francis, was displeased at the news, I could tell, but he said nothing and the conversation went on to other things.

The next morning, however, when I was helping him to wash, he said to me, "Leo, I could not sleep last night very well for our 'Song of the Creatures'"—he never said "my" for anything if he could avoid it—"our 'Song of the Creatures' kept running through my mind. I've added another stanza to it. See what you think." And he began to sing with a soft but true voice the verses he had composed:

All praise be yours, my Lord, through those who
*   grant pardon*
For love of you; through those who endure
Sickness and trial.
Happy those who endure in peace,
By you, Most High, they will be crowned.

"That is lovely, Francis," I said. "You were thinking about the bishop and the mayor, weren't you? It is too bad they cannot hear it. It might heal their anger and bring them to be friends again."

"You are right, Leo, I was thinking about them, but I was thinking about me, too. Anger is another type of sickness we humans suffer. The bishop, the mayor, I, all of us carry the heavy weight of our fallen human nature, prone to sin. But Jesus lifts that weight from us so there is hope, and where there is hope, there is joy; and where there is joy there ought to be a song. So let us sing the song together." So we did, with as much gusto as we could.

"Do you know, little lamb, you had an excellent idea. The bishop and the mayor ought to hear our song. Maybe their hearts would be touched and they would forgive each other. Ask Angelo to come to see me."

Angelo, before becoming a friar, had been a minstrel at city fairs. He still loved to sing and play the lute at any occasion, even without any occasion. He was one of the brothers assigned to beg for the Poor Ladies right there at San Damiano, so I went off looking for him and told him that Francis wanted him to come and to bring his lute.

When he arrived, Francis explained, "Angelo, you recall our 'Song of the Creatures' which we sang together at Sacro Speco a few years ago. I think that I mentioned then that I thought that the song was not finished, that there might be more to it. During the night the Lord gave me another stanza. Listen."

He began the "Song" from the beginning:

Most high, all-powerful, all good, Lord!
All praise is yours, all glory, all honor
And all blessing.

We sang it together, Angelo accompanying us on the lute, and then when we came to what had been the end, Francis and I continued with the new stanza.

"Can you remember that, Angelo?" he asked. "Do you want us to sing it again?"

"No, Francis, I have it. That is lovely. I will sing it to Sister Clare and the other sisters."

"Not now, Angelo. Later," he answered. "Right now I have an errand for you. I want you to take your lute and go to the city hall. There I want you to say this to the mayor: 'Sir mayor, Brother Francis, your servant, has sent me to you. He asks that you accompany me to the bishop's residence right now.' I think he will go with you. When you get to the bishop's residence, I want you to say: 'My Lord Bishop, Brother Francis has sent me to you and to the mayor. He asks that you listen to the song that the Lord has given to him.' Then sing our song for them, and when you come to the latest stanza be sure that you are looking at them, so that they will understand the words. Now go. Leo and I will be praying for you here that your singing and our song might bring peace to the two of them."

Angelo told us later that when the bishop and the mayor heard the "Song of the Creatures" they both started to weep. And when it had ended, the mayor asked the bishop for his forgiveness, which the bishop gave; then the bishop asked the mayor to forgive him, too, and they embraced each other as friends.

The final verse of the song was added about two weeks later, about the beginning of September. The weather had begun to change a bit, the summer heat lessening and cooler air coming down off Mount Subasio during the night. The fields of wheat were changing color. I mentioned the fact to Francis, "The farmers will soon be starting the harvest: the wheat, the grapes, the olives. It is a wonderful time of the year, Francis."

"Yes, it is time for the gathering of what has been sown, Leo. And after the harvest, a time of rest. I do not think I will see the grapes gathered this year, little lamb. The Lord will have gathered me into his barn by then."

"But Francis, the grape harvest is only a month away! Surely you don't think you will have gone to the Lord by then?"

"I do, Leo. By this time next month I will be with the Lord. And I tell you, my friend, that I am looking forward to it with joy. Just think! Not only will I be in the Heavenly Court with Jesus and our Blessed Lady, but also with our dear Brother Peter Catanii, with our brothers who gave up their lives for the faith in Africa, with all the holy angels and saints. And from there I will be able to do far more for the brothers than I can do here, limited as I am by my illness. So please don't try to hold me back nor should you feel sad, for we were born to live for God, to die with God, and to be with

God in eternity. I have done all that I can here."

The next morning, when I was helping Francis to wash himself, he said to me, "Leo, ask Angelo to come here this morning so that we can sing our song."

Angelo brought his lute and we sang the "Song of the Creatures." But when we reached the last verse, Francis, in his soft voice, a smile on his face, continued on. Angelo accompanied him.

> *All praise be yours, my Lord, through Sister*
>   *Death,*
> *From whose embrace no mortal can escape.*
> *Woe to those who die in mortal sin!*
> *Happy those she finds doing your will!*
> *The second death can do no harm to them.*
> *Praise and bless my Lord, and give him thanks,*
> *And serve him with great humility.*

The last note hung in the air for a moment before it died.

"There, our song is finished," he whispered. "Life is a song, a splendid melody. God gives it to us to sing it for a moment, but our rendition comes to an end, our song is over and someone else takes up the song. You, Leo, you, Angelo, must continue the song and teach our song to others who will come after us. Will you? Do you promise?"

My eyes filled with tears and I heard Angelo sob. I couldn't find my voice, so I whispered, "Yes, we promise."

How does word get about? I told no one and I am

sure Angelo would not, but somehow the mayor heard that Francis had written another stanza to the song and that it was about death. He was sure that Francis was near death! What to do? Certainly he could not leave Francis there in that hut outside the walls, he thought. What if he dies there? What if someone should come from Perugia, or anywhere, and take away his body? He was a son of Assisi! He belonged to Assisi, not anywhere else. Something had to be done!

So two days later a group of knights, led by the mayor, showed up at the little house outside the walls of San Damiano. No, they would not take "no" for an answer. It was unseemly, they said, that their neighbor, their native son, should not get better care. There were doctors, good doctors in the city, who would see to him. He should be in a proper house, a decent bed, not in this hut exposed to the damp and who knows what dangers. No, it was decided by the commune that Francis would be better off in Assisi.

I saw that it was useless to resist. They were intent on having it their way. So I said, "Give us a moment to prepare him. He is too weak to even ride a mule so he'll have to go by litter."

"We have a litter," one of them said.

I went into the hut where Francis was lying in the darkness. "Francis," I explained, "the mayor and some knights have come to take you to Assisi. They say they will be able to give you better treatment there and you will be safer there."

"Dear Leo, you and Clare have cared for me very

well. Better than a poor beggar deserves. And we both know that I have little time left. But let it be so. Let me be as a captive in their hands. They mean well."

"But Francis, probably I won't be able to care for you anymore. They will have doctors and nurses, maybe guards at the door to protect you from who knows what. What if I can't get to see you when I need to talk to you?"

"Leo, bring a pen and paper and a candle so that you can see to write." When I had found everything, he said, "Leo, we have known each other almost all our lives. You joined me and the others when we were only a handful; you have been a constant support and friend all these years. On many of the tours to preach the gospel you and I have been together, so that there is hardly a journey that I have made without you. And the longest journey of them all, this journey of life, you have been a part of that. Now that our journey is coming to an end I am not going to abandon you nor be inaccessible to you. Now, write down what I tell you:

Brother Leo, send greetings and peace to your Brother Francis.

As a mother to her child, I speak to you, my son. In this one word, this one piece of advice, I want to sum up all that we said on our journey, and, in case hereafter you still find it necessary to come to me for advice, I want to say this to you: In whatever way you think you will best please our Lord God and follow in his footsteps and in poverty, take that way with the Lord God's bless-

*ing and my obedience. And if you find it neces-
sary for your peace of soul or your own consola-
tion and you want to come to me, Leo, then come.
Keep that, little lamb of God, dear Leo, and never
lose it.*

I have kept that note from Francis all these years, carrying it always with me, but I know that the time will
come for me soon that I will be with Francis in heaven
where I will have no need of it. We will see each other
face to face, heart to heart.

CHAPTER

❧6❧

AT THE END OF SEPTEMBER I heard that Francis was coming down to St. Mary of the Angels where I had been living since he went up to Assisi from San Damiano. He had sent word to Brother Elias, saying that his time was near and that he wanted to depart from this world from his favorite place on earth. Some friars were sent with a litter to carry Francis to the infirmary that had been made ready for him behind and off to the right of the little church he had repaired close to twenty years before.

I and many of the other friars walked up the road toward Assisi to meet him and we waited for him outside the leprosarium where he and many of us had cared for the unfortunate patients inside. Out of the lower gate of the city and down the slope came a retinue of friars, some carrying the litter on which lay Francis. Laypeople and some knights on horseback added a touch of splendor to the sad procession and also some protection.

As the group approached where we were gathered, waiting, we all burst into a spontaneous applause, as for a visiting king or hero. And many called out *"Viva*

Francesco" and "*Viva il Poverello*," "Long live Francis, Long live the little poor one!" I found myself laughing and crying, both at once, and with many of the others pushing and shoving to get close to him. "Francis, Francis," I cried. "Oh how I've missed you!"

"Leo, Leo, is that you? Come, help me."

"What, Francis? What can I do?"

"Have the brothers turn the litter around so that I might see, for the last time, my beloved Assisi." We turned the litter so that he was facing back to the city from which he had come. "Now, Leo, lift me up a bit, that I might bless it."

I put my arm under his frail shoulders and lifted him up a little. His face turned upward toward the city which lay in a blackness beyond his ability to see, he lifted a hand and in the air made the Sign of the Cross. "God bless you, Mother Assisi," he prayed. "You have given life to many, saints and sinners, and offered shelter to all who came to you. May the good God protect you in the future from war and disease, leading you along the paths of peace. Amen."

"Amen," all of us said who could hear his blessing. The bearers picked up the litter as Francis lay back on the pallet and closed his eyes. There, inside of his eyes, I suspected, was a vision of the city he had just blessed; a remembrance of how it appeared years ago on that day when as a young man he had met, at this very spot, a leper, and instead of rushing off in fright and disgust he had dismounted to embrace the leper. On that day he had overcome his fears, he had overcome himself, he had embraced Christ. And today he was saying good-bye to that part of his life that had been, giving it his blessing and turning bravely to what yet lay ahead.

At St. Mary of the Angels Francis lay in the infirmary and waited for Sister Death to come for him. He had dictated his last testament and I had dutifully written it down, which he asked to have read at all gatherings of the brothers whenever they read the Rule of Life that he had given us. He lay on a mat on the flagstone floor of the infirmary. His frail body did not raise the threadbare blanket much above the level of the mat. Outside the window some doves were carrying on a guttural conversation among themselves and I was slowly wiping the ink from the point of the quill, tidying up the writing kit, for I was loathe to leave him.

"Leo, little lamb of God," he murmured, turning his head toward where I sat on the floor next to him. "This is the day I will leave this homeland for the one the good God promised to us. But before that moment comes, dear Leo, I want you to do me a favor."

"Of course, Francis, anything."

"Leo, we have been not only brothers now for many years, but friends as well. You and I have shared much together and perhaps, next to Sister Clare, you know me better than anyone. You know how much I love Umbria and this valley, the city of Assisi. Here I came to know God in a special way and he brought me to the knowledge of him through the works of his hands here where I was born and now, I thank him, where I am dying. If I will miss anything in heaven, Leo, it will be

Umbria. I am not able to do this, Leo, so I'm asking you to do it for me: Go up to Assisi. Go to the fort, the Rocca Maggiore, and climb up to the highest tower. And there, Leo, look out on Assisi. Fill your eyes, for me, since I cannot any longer fill my own, with the town: the pigeons circling in the *piazza comune*, the sun shining on the bell tower of San Rufino, the embracing walls that protected us so often from harm. Look out over the valley where the smoke rises slowly from the burning stubble of the fields, the afternoon sun shines on farmers' ponds and the oak trees of the woods seem so black. Smell for me, Leo, one last time the perfume of grass drying in the sun and the aroma of the wood fires from the chimneys of the town. Listen for me to the song of the lark and to the sigh of the breeze in the poplars nearby. Feel for me the warmth of the sun as it lowers toward the west and touch the stones of the tower, cut from the side of Mount Subasio. Fill your being with all of that, Leo, and shout to God, for me, 'I thank you, Lord. In the name of your little one, Francis, I thank you for your blessings, for Umbria, for Assisi.' And when you have done this, come back here to me. I will not leave until you return."

"Francis," I whispered, "are you afraid to die?" It was a silly question, but I felt that I had to ask it.

"Afraid, Leo? Afraid to die? Years ago, when we were young, I might have been. When we were just starting out on this great adventure of ours. There were times, I think, when I feared leaving no trace of my passing through this world, of being a sterile plant dropping no seeds in this fertile Umbrian earth for future growth. I was afraid at one time that my life, and my death, would be meaningless. But not now, Leo. I have lived beyond that. Even though I see that my life *has* made a difference, that is not important to me now. It is my ultimate poverty, I think, that I ask for nothing, want nothing, count on nothing. Whatever God wants for me, that is enough and that is everything. No, if I were afraid of anything, it might be that I would be afraid *not* to die. Ever since those days when you and I used to go up to the caves at the Carceri, when we were both praying to know God's will and he revealed it to me in such a simple way, I have been waiting for this moment of life. I realized, and you did, too, that time was brief here on earth and that it should not be thrown away on foolish things. Every minute of every day I have tried to grasp life in my hands, squeezing from it the juice of life, drinking it down, not wasting a drop. Even though I didn't let Brother Body grow fat on food, I nourished my spirit with the presence and the reality of God, picking him like a berry from the bushes of creation. My poor body has grown weak, like a dry pod, and it's ready to cast the seed of my spirit into the autumn air. I am ready, Leo. I need to have this life over and to make sense of it, to die. So go. Leave me here. I will wait for you to fill my being with my beloved Umbria, and then it will be over."

So I went. As I trudged up the slope toward the western gate, looking up to Assisi above the olive trees, it was difficult to see the city clearly because of the tears that came to my eyes. How often Francis and I, Francis and other friars, Francis alone, had come up this road from St. Mary of the Angels! I turned around and looked back along the road. The church of St. Mary, the huts of the friars, the infirmary where Francis lay dying were hidden among the oak trees. The sun shone warmly on the valley, making the autumn colors of the fields stand out. "Shouldn't it be overcast, the sun refusing to shine?" I thought. "No, those are my own feelings, not Francis'. He is joyous to the end, and it's right that the sun shine brightly on his death."

Turning, I went through the city gate and started climbing the steps that would bring me to the main square by the temple of Minerva and then on up to the fort. The way led me past the Bernardone shop where years before Francis had worked for his father. Angelo, Francis' brother, who now owned the shop, stood outside in the warm sunshine. We had known each other since childhood when both my parents worked as weavers for his father.

"Peace to you, Angelo," I said, stopping in front of him. He was unmistakably Francis' brother, but much heavier. The business evidently provided a good table. "How are you and the family?"

"We're all well, Brother Leo, thank you. Are you out begging today? I don't really have anything to spare right now. The times are not good for us business people, you know. I can't afford to give anything away these days. Not any cloth, anyhow. If you need a loaf of bread or something like that, maybe Elvira, the wife, would have something to spare. You can knock at the door around the corner. How is my brother Francis? I hear he has not been feeling well lately."

"Well, thank you for the offer of the bread, Angelo, but I'm not out begging. I'm just passing by here on my way to the fort. As for Francis, he is dying. Weren't you aware of that? I thought everyone knew. It's a lucky thing, then, that I saw you. You'll want to get down to St. Mary's to be with him, I'm sure."

"I'm sorry to hear that, Brother. Actually I am all alone here today at the shop. I can't get away right now. Maybe later." With that he turned and went back into the shop.

There, I thought, is one of the mysteries of life. How can two people, from the same family, be so unlike? Francis so aware of God and caring nothing for the things of this world. Angelo so aware of this world and caring nothing for God. Would Francis have been the same if God had not forcibly intervened? Some people thought him a saint. Yes, I think the seed of goodness, the sense of God, was always there and he would have been a good, a decent man in any event. But the fact was that God did call him to an extraordinary life, and the rest of us merely watched him with our mouths open.

Turning up the street from the *piazza comune* toward the cathedral, I saw Brother Bernard hurrying in my direction.

"Oh, thank God I came upon you, Leo," he said, out of breath. "No one seems to know anything. How is

Francis? I had an overpowering urge to get down to St. Mary of the Angels to see him. I should be there with him. What news do you have of him?"

I had to smile at him and that in itself seemed to calm him. Bernard, who lived a hermit's life at the Carceri, had probably just spoken more words at one time than he had all year.

"I am sorry, Bernard," I replied. "I guess no one thought to send up word to you and the others that Francis is dying. But evidently God has supplied what we failed to do, to call you down to Francis' side. He will want you there to give you a blessing before he leaves us."

"But Leo, if he is so close to death, what are you doing here, going in the other direction?"

"I'm on an errand for him, Bernard. Up to the fort. Come with me, then we will both go back to Francis. There is time."

"An errand to the fort? Now? What do you have to do there? There's nobody there. It's abandoned."

"I know, but come with me. I'll try to explain as we go, and then we'll go back to him."

We walked by the alley that led to my family's home. One of my brothers lived there still, with his family. But I had no time now to stop. Turning to the left we climbed the steep steps that led to the fort. It had been abandoned for several years now and many of the stones used for the building of the city walls had come from its own walls.

As we went I told Bernard what my errand was,

how Francis longed to fill his being with the smell and sight of Assisi, as though he would take a part of it to heaven with him. Bernard nodded; I could see that he understood exactly, and tears formed in his eyes, spilling over to run down his cheeks.

"I know, Leo. And you know, too, perhaps even better than I, how much Francis loves this part of the world. In a way, he *is* Assisi. And Assisi is Francis."

We came to the open space beneath the walls of the fort. The gate stood open, sagging on its hinges.

"You go in, Leo," Bernard said. "I'll wait here for you."

I found my way to the very top of the keep and there, as Francis had directed me, I looked down on the town, on the valley, at the mountains behind me. This was my home, too, and I loved it: the tiled roofs of the homes crouching on the hillside, the soft call to prayer from a convent bell, the haze fading off toward blue hills in the distance. Here Francis had found God, and God had found Francis. Now God was taking him from these olive trees and poplars to an even better place, but I could not go with him this time as I had so often followed him in the past.

Not yet.

Oh, Francis, I thought. Life here is going to be so empty without you! But because of you my own life has been so different from what it might have been! Thank you. And I thank you, too, God, for lending him to this town, this valley, and to me.

Taking a last look out over the city, I turned and ran

down the steps. I motioned to Bernard, who fell in beside me, and we hurried down through the alleys and stairways toward the road leading to St. Mary of the Angels. We had to get back to Francis before sundown, I was sure, and already the sun was getting close to the horizon.

The street wound past Bernard's family home. Someone else lived there now these many years since he had sold it, given the money to the poor and joined Francis at San Damiano. He noticed me looking at it.

"A lot has happened since I sold it and threw in my lot with Francis, hasn't it? To both of us!"

"Yes, Bernard. You were the first to join him. Do you regret it?"

"Regret it? No, Leo, not a bit. Not that it has been easy. Well, at first it was. It was a lark, an adventure, at first, living there at San Damiano, rebuilding the chapel. It was heroic, you know? And it was exciting when John the Simple joined us, and then Peter Catanii and Giles. We went off to Florence, remember? You wanted to come and Francis wouldn't let you. Yes, it was an adventure, all right. But then reality set in, the realization of what I had done; there was the daily hardship of poverty. But regret it? No. When it was hardest to continue, there was the example of Francis to encourage me. Next to God, I owe everything to him."

"How did you come to the decision to join him, Bernard?"

"Well, as you know, I had been on a pilgrimage to the Holy Land. When I returned here to Assisi I found that our one-time *bon vivant* and party-goer was living at San Damiano, that he begged stones for his project and begged for his food, too. Most of his former friends were convinced that he had gone crazy and dismissed him as someone to pity, to be laughed at. But I was not so sure. I thought maybe it was a temporary fervor with no real depth. So I asked him a few times to my home and suggested he spend the night there after we had stayed up for hours talking about the holy places, about the Gospels. Whenever he came he would not eat the meal I had prepared, but he would insist that we go out to the neighbors to beg for something to eat. I felt like a fool, of course. Can you imagine me asking old Signora Lucca next door for some bread and cheese? But people gave us things! We would bring it back to the house where we sat on the floor by the hearth and ate what we had begged. I swear it, Leo, it was delicious!

"Later, when we grew tired of talking, I would insist that he stay the night. Francis would make a show of yawning and make a bed for himself there by the fire with the blankets I gave him. He no sooner lay his head down than he would breathe heavily as though fast asleep. But I have to admit, Leo, that I spied on him. I had to know! When he thought I was asleep, Francis got up and, on his knees, spent the rest of the night praying. I know, I watched him! When it started to get light, only then did he lie down lest I discover him. And then he slept until I woke him at daylight. Then we would go to Mass together at San Masseo Church.

"I knew, Leo, that Francis was not a fool nor a charlatan. He was real. I went down to San Damiano a few times to help him with the work he was doing there. And after our work one morning I asked him, 'Francis, since coming home from my pilgrimage I have been asking God for direction in my life, but so far have no answer. What do you think I should do?'

"It was then that he suggested that we go to the Word of God for help. So after Mass one morning at San Masseo Church we asked the priest to show us a Bible. Francis and I prayed for guidance, then he had me open the book, close my eyes and put my finger on the page. When I had done that, he said, 'Read what God's will for you is.'

"I opened my eyes, saw that I had opened the Bible to Saint Matthew's Gospel and read the words which my finger indicated: 'Go, sell what you have, and give it to the poor.' And that, Leo, is what I did."

"But weren't you scared, Bernard? I remember what consternation that caused. You had a good bit of money, and some property, besides."

"At first I was scared. I admit it. But, as I said, I have learned. I have learned to put my hand into the hand of God and to step out into the darkness. That is what I learned from watching Francis. And that is what he is about to do now, for the last time. None of us knows what death is like nor what waits for us on the other side of life. But with our hand in the hand of God, we can take that step."

Arriving back at the infirmary, we found the whole

community gathering. The guardian of the friary grabbed both Bernard and me and led us to the door. "He has been asking for both of you," he whispered.

Francis lay upon the floor of the infirmary, a stone under his head. "He insisted," explained the guardian. "And when he is dead he says we must remove his habit and leave him to lie naked upon the floor for as long as it takes for a man to walk a mile slowly. Oh, Leo, I don't know if I can do it."

"Leo," murmured Francis, "is it you?"

"Yes, Francis, it is I. I am back."

"Is my first-born, my eldest son, here? Where is Bernard?"

"Here, Francis," Bernard whispered, kneeling down beside him.

"Bernard, let me bless you," Francis murmured with some difficulty, and he reached out his hand. Someone guided his hand to Bernard's bowed head. "Yes, yes, Bernard, it is you. May God bless you and keep you. May he turn his face to you and give you peace. God bless you. And Leo? Are you here, little lamb of God? Did you see? Did you look one last time? Did you breathe it all in for me?"

"Yes, my dear brother, one last time. For you," I assured him through my tears.

Francis opened his sightless eyes very wide as though looking out from the top of the fort upon his beloved Assisi and the valley of Umbria. He breathed in deeply, a smile lit up his face. He exhaled, his soul escaped to God.